TENNESSEE WHISKEY

EMMA BRAY

CHAPTER ONE

Nick

I ROLL down the window and breathe in the scent of freshly mown grass as I speed down the old state highway that now looks like some sort of backwoods backroad. Although it's humid and hot as hell in the southern atmosphere, the fresh, earthy smell of Tennessee is starting to put me in a slightly better mood. Just a little bit.

It sure beats the mechanical, polluted smell of Boston anyway.

The reporters. Always in my face, trying to twist anything into a scandal. Starting rumors.

Yeah, it's no wonder I have a permanent scowl on my face.

Of course, I still kept my house in the city, but it'll be nice to have this country house to get away to when I want a break, and I'm in desperate need of one right now.

As the owner of one of the biggest software companies on the globe, I can work from wherever I want. Yeah, there are certain meetings I have to conduct in person in the city, but there's no reason why I can't conduct some of them virtually too. The hell away from everybody.

And I gotten this mansion in Tennessee for a steal. What would normally be a thirty million dollar home in Boston I got for a mere two million. Not like I'm lacking in finances. I'm one of Boston's most eligible billionaire bachelors—a moniker than makes me scowl just thinking about it—but I'm a smart investor if nothing else, so I couldn't pass up on the deal when I came across it.

I've never lived in the country before. I was born in the city—with concrete under my feet and all that—but my folks were from around here, so I have some sort of relations in the area even if I've never explored them. Maybe it's time I connect with my roots and slow it down a bit. Get a breather from the hustle and bustle of the city.

I only wish my parents were here to share in my success. They died in a car crash when I was a teen, so they never got to see my rise to billionaire status, and they weren't here for me to buy them the home of their dreams in their hometown, so I guess I'm doing this partly in their honor.

I reach over to flick on the radio and grimace when the twang of country music filters through the air. I hurry to change the station. I might long for the solitude and beauty of the countryside, but that doesn't mean I enjoy the whining that is country music. My tastes are much more refined. I finally find a station playing some light instrumental and leave it there.

When my eyes flick back up to the road, I slam on the brakes with a curse and skid to a stop.

A young woman stands fearlessly in the middle of the road with her hand held up to stop traffic. Granted, I'm the only traffic around. There are no other cars on this otherwise deserted road, but still. Jesus, I could have run her over.

My chest heaves with the adrenaline of my heart jumping up into my chest in panic at the close call, but the girl seems unconcerned. Her fiery red hair curls all around her face and shoulders like a lioness' mane before falling down to her waist. It's unruly and wild, making her look like something untamed.

My eyes rove over her slim frame, from the baby blue tank top and faded cut-off shorts to the thin, tan-colored flip-flops on her feet with red-painted toenails.

I watch in fascination as she bends down and picks something up out of the middle of the road. When she straightens, I see what's held in her hand and give an incredulous bark of laughter.

A turtle. The girl risked her life to stop traffic and help a turtle cross the street.

I watch as her long legs walk deftly to the other side of the road where she sets the terrapin down on the grass well off the side of the pavement before giving his shell an affectionate pat. She stands and starts to cross the road again to get back into the beat up-looking white truck I've just now noticed sitting on the side of the road.

I lean out of my rolled-down window, "Seriously? You realize I could have run you over?" I ask her with a growl, irritated that she put her life at risk in such a way.

She pauses by my luxury rental car and looks into my eyes for the first time.

Her eyes are a cerulean blue, a stunning color combination with her red hair. Her skin is flawless and milky, not tan like I'd normally expect of southern girls. Her lips are pink and lush, and I can't stop the visceral and immediate reaction of my body to the whole package of her looking at me directly like this.

She's stunning, but it's more than that. Something I can't put my finger on. Something that causes my chest to squeeze and renders me incapable of tearing my eyes from her.

She shrugs down at me like the fact that she endangered herself so recklessly is no big deal. "He needed help," she states simply, her voice smooth and musical and utterly feminine and innocent at the same time.

Her nonchalant attitude snaps me back to the matter at hand. I frown at her. "Nevertheless, that was dangerous."

She frowns. "He's an innocent animal. Somebody had to save him from assholes like you who come speeding down the highway like a bat out of hell. I couldn't just let him get run over."

I blink at the dressing down she gives me and regard her curiously. I can't remember the last time someone talked to me that way. Even the city's most powerful men know better than to show me such disrespect. "You have no sense of self-preservation, do you?"

Her eyes flash at the reprimand, and she crosses her arms over her chest as she points out, "Standing here arguing this point with you is keeping me in the middle of the road."

I realize she might have a point there. She raises a delicate brow at me. I'm stopped in the middle of the road, detaining her from getting back into her shitty-looking truck and getting out of the potential line of traffic.

"Get out of the road," I order her, waiting until she frowns but moves to do as I say before I maneuver my car onto the side of the road behind her truck.

She stops with a hand on the door handle to her truck and looks back at me as I just sit there watching her. I think I might be freaking her out, but I just want to make sure she gets in her vehicle okay and that the piece of shit starts.

It looks dubious at best.

I make a motion at her through my windshield, urging her to go on, and her pretty little lips turn down into a scowl, obviously put off at a complete stranger like me ordering her around. I feel my lips twitch. She's a firecracker. In every way, from her sassy little attitude to that captivating mane of red hair.

I watch patiently as she yanks on the door of the

truck and then climbs up into the vehicle that looks way too big for a cute little thing like her.

If she were mine, I'd have her driving a sleek little Mercedes that would complement her but still provide plenty of safety.

She'd be wearing designer labels that would do her figure justice. I'd cover her with aquamarine diamonds that would only bring out the blue of her eyes.

My hands tighten on the steering wheel with the clarity of the images my mind conjures.

I don't know anything about this girl, but she looks like she should be *mine*.

I frown as I hear the turning of her truck's engine before it craps out. The fucker won't start. Just as I suspected. I honestly don't know how she drove it here in the first place. The piece of junk looks like it was on its last leg ten years ago.

I put my car into drive and pull up right beside her before putting it back in park. The window to the truck is rolled down. If I had to guess, I'd bet my last million it doesn't have working air conditioning in it. She eyes me suspiciously as I roll down the passenger side window before nodding to the seat next to me, "Get in," I tell her.

She stares at me from the inside of the truck before she scoffs, "Uh, yeah, no way, buddy."

Daisy

I watch his jaw tense as I tell him there's no way I'm getting into his car with him. He might be the most breathtaking man I've ever seen, but I don't know hide nor hair about him, and even the devil was supposedly God's most beautiful angel—that's what my gran says anyway.

His hair is dark and carelessly tousled in a stylish way. His arms look muscular beneath the dark button-up shirt he's wearing, the sleeves rolled-up to reveal strong forearms and a few buttons undone to reveal the top of his chest.

My heart thumped in my chest when he first spoke to me so moodily. A strange warmth filled my body at the deep timbre of his voice, but it was quickly tempered with annoyance at his sharp tone, ordering me about as if I'm a child.

Perhaps the most arresting thing about him, though, is his golden eyes. They're not brown, and they're not exactly amber. They're the most unique hue I've ever seen—in eyes anyway. They glimmer at me beneath his dark brows now as he frowns at me.

I think all the man knows how to do is glower and frown.

And order me around.

And treat me like I'm stupid for caring about the sanctity of animal life.

He curses, "I can't very well leave you here stranded."

"Don't worry about me," I retort back at him through our windows. "I'll be fine."

He runs a hand through his hair as he turns his head to glance out his sideview mirror before he suddenly slams his car into gear and shoots up in front of my truck, pulling his car into park off the side of the road in front of me.

I'm glued to the spot in shock as I watch the driver's side door open and see him step from the fancy vehicle with a long unfolding of limbs.

I gulp as he slams the door of his car shut and starts stalking over toward where I sit in my truck. My piece of crap truck that *would* choose today of all days to act up on me. I shouldn't have turned it off when I stopped to help the turtle cross the road. I should have just left it idling. I knew better. I knew that sometimes my ornery truck refused to start. Stupid, stupid, stupid!

I suddenly realize the danger of my situation. I'm stranded on the side of the road with a total stranger.

My dumb self forgot to grab my cell phone before I left the house, something that I do frequently. I never really worry about it, though, when I'm just going to see my gran. She's about a seven-minute drive from where I live with my parents.

I consider jumping out of my truck and running. Maybe that would be the sensible thing to do, but I'm too stubborn and have too much pride to run. If the devil is coming for me, I'll meet him head on, and I sure as hell won't go down without a fight.

I sit up straighter in my seat and glare at the man defiantly as he finally reaches my truck.

He leans into my truck with an arm on the top of the window, his golden eyes boring into mine, seeming to burn me with their heat at such close range.

My breath catches in my throat despite myself. Instead of feeling fear, though, as I probably should, I feel this keen sense of excitement.

He stares at me for a long moment. I feel his eyes scorching every inch of my skin as they travel over my face. The intensity in his gaze is unnerving, like he's trying to see deep inside me to my soul.

"I just want to make sure you get home okay." His eyes seem to soften, and he suddenly looks more approachable, less brooding.

I still don't trust him for a minute.

"You're not from around here, are you?" I don't know why I ask it. It's obvious he's an out-of-towner. Everybody knows everybody around here, so the fact that I've never seen the guy lets me know with absolute certainty that he's not from around here.

And I'd certainly remember if I'd ever seen anyone like *him* before. He looks like one of those guys you see on the movies or the covers of magazines. His clothes look perfectly tailored to him and probably cost more than my parent's monthly mortgage.

His gaze never falters from me, but his lips finally quirk up in the semblance of a smile. Or perhaps it's more of a smirk.

"Not yet," he says by way of answer.

I frown at him, tilting my head to the side as I consider his odd answer. His eyes are still holding mine, but I'm broken from the golden trance of them when I hear the whooshing of a vehicle coming around the corner.

I look up just as I see Jake's brand-new truck rounding the corner. I see the stranger's gaze following mine to the truck, and his frown deepens as it slows when Jake obviously notices my truck sitting on the side of the road.

I feel an odd mixture of relief and disappointment at the appearance of a friendly face who can help me. I don't really know where the disappointment is coming from because there's no way in hell I was ever going to get into a car with this man I don't even know. My childhood friend showing up couldn't have been better timing.

"Daisy!" Jake rolls down his window and yells at me with his boyish grin.

"Daisy," I hear the dark-haired man repeat my name thoughtfully as if he's trying it out for size. I feel his stare on me, but I ignore him and the heat that flushes my face as I call back to Jake, "Hey, Jake!"

"The old girl crap out on you again?" Jake asks me knowingly. Yeah, he's picked me up more than once when my truck wouldn't start.

"Yeah," I nod as I open the door of my truck. The stranger steps back just in time to avoid the swing of my truck door smacking him as I hop out.

I can feel him scowling again, but I continue to ignore him. I'm not purposefully trying to be rude, but Mr. Grouchy Pants has done nothing but stare and glower at me since I met him, and I'm already over it.

I run over to Jake's truck and hop into the passenger side. I see my sandy-haired friend looking at the dark-haired man curiously.

"Who's that?" he asks, making no move to hide his interest in the stranger.

I shrug, not even glancing back at whatever-his-name-is. I feel a pang when I realize I don't even know his name, but then I realize it's probably for the best. He's just someone passing through, and I'll surely never see him again.

"Just someone who stopped to see what was going on."

Jake frowns. "Good thing I showed up when I did then. You don't need to be taking rides from strangers, Daisy," he warns.

"I know," I agree with him. "I wasn't going to."

"I don't think he would have hurt me, though," I can't help adding.

Jake looks at me quizzically, but thankfully he doesn't say anything about my odd comment. Instead, he just nods to the dark-haired guy before he pulls away from the curb and starts off down the road.

I chance a glance in the sideview mirror back at the man still standing by my truck on the side of the road. His jaw is clenched, his eyes boring into us as we drive away, his hands fisted at his sides.

I feel a shiver run up my spine despite the summer heat.

It's definitely a good thing Jake came along when he did.

CHAPTER TWO

Nick

I'M FUMING as I stalk back to my rental and hop inside. It's not the way she coldly ignored me, effectively dismissing me, that has my blood roiling in my veins.

It's the way she ran to that other man, the relief evident in her eyes. The southern punk with the sun-bleached hair, tanned skin, and golden boy smile.

I've never hated another man on sight so much.

And my reaction is ludicrous, I know. I have no claim on her. I don't even know her last name. She doesn't even know my first name. We didn't even have time to introduce ourselves before he came rolling up.

Yet, I find myself wanting to yank her out of his truck and tear him limb from limb.

I run my hands through my hair in irritation as I speed down the highway, my earlier peace rent in two at the thought of the little redhead's pretty blue eyes gazing up into Golden Boy's.

Daisy.

A pretty name for a pretty little wildflower. Maybe her name should be Rose or Ruby or Scarlet because of her red hair, but Daisy somehow fits her better. I've never met a Daisy before in my entire life, but somehow the name suits her. Unique. Like her.

It's stupid. It's crazy. But I torture myself of images of her and him the whole way to my new home. He's probably her fucking boyfriend. I shouldn't care about that, but I do.

Because as insane as it is I can't shake the territorial feeling that overwhelmed me when my eyes first met hers. Like she's *mine* to possess.

I shake my head before pinching between my brow and blowing out a breath, one hand still on the wheel. I'm supposed to be here to unwind—not shoot my blood pressure through the roof obsessing over some girl who saves turtles from road traffic.

I should just forget about her. Let her live her life, and I'll live mine.

But I know that as soon as I reach my destination, I'll be pulling out all my most advanced software to find out everything I can about the little redhead from Tennessee who would dare to walk away from Nick Amorini like he's nobody.

***

Daisy

"Thanks, Jake," I tell my best friend as I hop out of his truck into the gravel driveway of the only home I've ever known. The little two-story cottage-style house my parents bought when they were barely more than my age and pregnant with me looks picturesque sitting against the backdrop of the wooded greenery behind it and the setting sun. The white vinyl, black shutters, and white picket fence lining the front porch only serve to make it look even more homey. Pink and white azaleas line the front porch, and a white dogwood tree sits over to the side of the house. I've spent many an evening reading under that old tree.

"I'll have the truck brought over as soon as Uncle Don can manage it," Jake tells me.

My heart swells. Jake is the best friend a girl could ever have. I can't count how many times he's had his uncle pull my old truck off the side of the road and bring it home to me like a lost puppy.

"What would I do without you, Jakey?" I ask him playfully.

He crooks a grin at me. "You'd be stranded on the side of the road for one thing," he notes wryly.

I laugh. "True." My mind flits back to the dark-haired stranger with the piercing golden eyes. Somehow I don't think he'd have settled for leaving me on the side of the road. Something about him makes my insides knot up, though, so I'm thankful Jake showed up when he did.

"We still on for fishing Friday morning?" Jake asks.

"Sure," I tell him, casting a glance behind Jake's truck over to the pond I can just barely see glistening across the field that separates Mom and Dad's property from our neighbor's.

I've heard Mr. McEwen was planning on selling the place. He's owned the land adjacent to ours for all my life, and he never minded Jake and I playing on his land and swimming and fishing in his pond.

He has at least a hundred acres. He's one of the only millionaires around here. Just last year, he married a much younger woman and built a mansion just for her. Unfortunately, their marriage didn't work out. Apparently, she ran off to Florida with the gardener, and now poor Mr. McEwen can't stand to be in the home that reminds him of the young wife who betrayed him so brutally.

I don't blame him.

I seriously doubt if he'll ever sell the mansion, though. It's been on the market for over a year. Nobody around here has that kind of money, and there isn't really any industry or anything around here to draw the types of people who *do* have that type of money.

"Poor Mr. McEwen," Jake mutters as he follows my gaze over to the pond. The look on my face must have let him know what I was thinking of. We both love old Mr. McEwen like he's our own grandpa and hate what happened to him.

"Yeah," I sigh. "We should go pay him a visit soon."

"Yeah," Jake nods, agreeing with me. "Maybe we can swing by after we go fishing on Friday."

"Sounds like a plan," I nod and then wave at Jake as he finally rolls up his window in favor of the air conditioning before backing up out of our driveway.

Instead of going immediately into the house, I walk across our yard over to the old barbed wire fence serving as the boundary between our property and Mr. McEwen's.

I deftly swing my leg through the gap between the middle and third wire and then follow through with my torso to pass through the fence without a scratch in a practiced move I've been doing my whole life.

I make my way over to the edge of the pond and slip off my flip-flops. Although it's not as hot as it was earlier today, the heat this evening is still oppressive. I can feel my curls sticking to my neck, and the water is calling to me like a siren.

I don't even glance around me before shucking down to my bra and panties and diving in. Nobody ever comes out here but Jake and me. I can't count how many midnight swims I've taken in this pond over the years. It's like my own natural swimming pool.

I float on my back for a bit and look up at the clouds streaked with pink, purple, and amber as the sun begins to go down. I can just hear my gran warning me about cottonmouths if she could see me now. She'd freak if she knew just how much I go swimming in this pond. While I know that cottonmouth snakes are a real danger around any body of water here in Tennessee, I've never seen one here at the pond. It's like the universe knows this pond is my getaway and is expressly protecting me from the poisonous vipers.

I swim and float around until I can see the first flicker of light from the fireflies. Gran calls them light-ning bugs, but I like fireflies. It makes them sound more mystical that way.

The cicadas are starting to hum their summertime song by the time I climb out of the pond and lay in the grass while I dry off. This is something else Gran would reprimand me for. She'd say I'll be covered in ticks from laying in the grass like this, but I've pulled hundreds of ticks off me in my lifetime whether I lay in the grass or not. The fact is just walking outside this time of year is enough to get one on you. So far, I've been lucky and haven't come down with Rocky Moun-tain Spotted Fever or Lyme disease, though I know people who have.

Plus, there's no keeping Jake and me out of the woods. When we were little, we practically lived in them, seeing who could climb the highest in the trees. I always won. Jake said I was a regular monkey. I quirk a grin remembering our childhood antics. He was always just jealous I could out-climb him any day.

Still can.

I give a tiny laugh.

"What's so funny?"

My eyes fly open, and I jump to a sitting position, my hands coming up to cross over my chest to try to hide my bra-and-panty-clad form from the deep voice that I instantly recognize.

As soon as I look up, I see him.

The man from the side of the road. A lock of dark hair falls onto his forehead as he gazes down at me. He looks even taller towering over me like this, his golden eyes glowing in the dusk.

I scramble back to my feet and hurry to pull on my shorts and tank, never mind that my bra and panties are still damp and are getting my clothes wet.

"How long have you been standing there?" I ask him angrily.

He shrugs with a smirk and a vague, "Not long."

I scowl at him while I run my fingers through my damp curls. "What are you? Some sort of peeping tom?"

He chuckles at that before saying, "How can I be a peeping tom if it's my property?"

My eyes widen at that. "*You* bought Mr. McEwen's place?" I ask, dumbfounded.

It suddenly makes sense why I've never seen him before, why his clothing looks so expensive. God, I'm so stupid not to have put it together before.

"I guess so," he answers nonchalantly, never taking his eyes off me. The way he trains them on me makes my skin prickle with awareness.

I try to ignore the feeling as I focus on what he said. I feel a sinking feeling as I realize my days of coming to this pond are over. It belongs to *him* now. This guy who looks too rich for this setting.

"That still doesn't give you the right to stalk women," I lash out at him in my frustration. He's just unknowingly turned my entire world upside down, and I'm pissed that he'd been watching me in my underthings for god knows how long.

He laughs as if what I said was hilarious. The sound is deep and masculine, and it makes my toes curl where I still stand in the grass barefooted.

"If there's any crime being committed here, Daisy, it's trespassing." The way he says my name makes my heart skip a beat. He says it like his tongue caresses over every syllable, and the way his eyes seem to darken to amber when he looks at me makes me wonder if he's imagining his tongue caressing over more than just my name.

The thought makes my legs tremble, but I won't allow myself to show any nerves around him.

I raise my chin defiantly. "I am not a criminal. Mr. McEwen gave me permission to use his pond whenever I wish. I wasn't aware the place had been sold yet," I admit that last bit bitterly.

"How old are you?" he asks suddenly as he continues to study me.

He catches me so off guard that I answer him without thinking, "Eighteen."

"So, you're legally old enough to be tried as an adult," he notes.

My eyes widen, and my heart begins to race at the thought of being arrested, but then I see the twinkle of humor in his eyes, and my scowl deepens.

Earlier today he did nothing but scowl at me. I hate that he's turned the tables so that now I'm the one permanently scowling.

"I'm sorry for trespassing on your land. I'll just be on my way, and it won't happen again." I try to muster as much dignity as I can, standing tall as I deliver my edict. Although it pains me to apologize to him since he's the one who was spying on me, I do it anyway.

I start to walk in the direction of my parents' home, but he steps in my way, blocking my path.

I look up at him, noting the faint stubble on his jawline that only serves to enhance the angular lines of his face. He's wearing that same dark button-up shirt he was wearing earlier, and my eyes can't help being drawn to the exposed bit of his chest peeking out from the undone buttons. I quickly avert my eyes, praying to god he didn't catch me ogling his chest. It should be against the law for a man to be as handsome as he is.

"I'll forgive the offense on one condition," he says.

My eyes flick up to him in a mixture of annoyance and trepidation. I already said I was sorry. What more could the man want?

I cross my arms over my chest and raise an eyebrow at him, waiting.

He smiles devilishly, the full force of all his teeth showing mesmerizing. The man belongs on a magazine cover. I swear.

"Have dinner with me tomorrow night."

I stare at him disbelievingly before I give a nervous laugh even as my heart speeds up, "You can't be serious. I don't even know your name."

"Nick," he supplies his name immediately, those golden eyes never leaving me as he gazes down at me. I don't know how old this guy is, but I think it's safe to say he's more experienced than I am. *Guy* isn't even the right term for him. He's a *man* if I ever saw one.

A dangerous-looking man. The kind of man that daddies warn their daughters about. He vibrates with a dangerous sexuality like he can make girls drop their panties with one smoldering look.

And I am not about to be another notch in his belt. Nope. No way.

Nick

"Well, Nick," she enunciates my name sassily with a toss of her head, "I realize we're going to be neighbors now, but I don't think so."

Everything about her captivates me. Her fiery spirit, the way she fights me every step of the way.

She's nothing like the women who throw themselves at me once they find out my name and how much money I've got.

Something tells me even if I told her my last name, she wouldn't give a shit. Hell, she might not even recognize it.

That's more fucking freeing that I ever thought it could be.

My dick's been hard ever since I came upon her floating around in my pond in her bra and panties. They're white and simple, yet they look so perfect clinging to her wet skin, that flaming red hair fanned out around her in the water like she's a mermaid or something.

"Say it again," I order her.

Her little brow furrows as she clarifies, "There's no way I'm going to have dinner with you."

"Not that part," I shake my head at her.

Her little brow furrows adorably.

"My name," I clarify when she looks up at me in confusion like I'm crazy or something. Hell, maybe I am, but I don't care. I can't explain this need to hear my name coming from her lips again. "Say my name again."

She takes a step back from me, eyeing me warily. Shit, I'm scaring the hell out of her.

I take a deep breath and run my hand through my hair, tearing my gaze away from her perfect form for just a moment to try to get ahold of myself before I do something really stupid—like sling her over my shoulder like a caveman and take her back to my house.

"Please?" I force the word from my lips. It's not one I'm used to saying. I'm used to people jumping to obey my orders, but I'll ask nicely for her.

"Nick," she says softly. I close my eyes at the sound. God, I want to hear her screaming it while I eat her pussy until her legs shake. "I need to go home," she continues.

"I'll pick you up at seven," I tell her.

She gives an incredulous laugh. "I thought I said no, Nick." She says my name again, like now that she's said it she can taunt me with it.

"Pity," I say, willing to play hardball if she is. "I didn't want to call the cops on my neighbors my first day in town."

Her eyes widen before they narrow again as she spears me with her icy blue gaze, "You wouldn't dare."

I step up to her until there's barely an inch of space between us and she has to crane her head up to look at me. I can smell the flowery scent wafting up from her damp hair. She smells like honeysuckle, and I wonder if it's from whatever shampoo she uses or if that's just her natural scent. My eyes rove over her hair that falls down to her waist. The curls are already tightening up into ringlets as they dry. I want to run my fingers through them, but I don't.

"Try me," I warn her.

Granted, I wouldn't really call the cops on her, but if letting her believe I would is what gets her to agree to spend time with me, then I'm not above misleading her.

I didn't get to where I am without being a bit of a cutthroat. Like a shark, I've always been able to smell blood and know just how to get what I want, and I'm not above using whatever means necessary to do it. That's what makes my business ventures so successful.

If I have to deploy those same skills with her, then so be it.

She huffs out a breath and looks away before she looks back up at me suspiciously. "Why are you doing this?"

I answer her honestly, "I'm used to getting what I want."

She scoffs and asks, "And what do you want?"

I decide to lay all my cards on the table. "You, Daisy."

Her eyes are as wide as saucers as she stares up at me. I've finally rendered her speechless. I reach out to trail a finger along her jawline, feeling how petal soft her skin is. I give in to the urge to finger one of her curls, taking it between my thumb and forefinger.

Her tongue darts out to lick her lips, drawing my attention to their plushness.

Christ...

I make myself take a step back from her before I act on what I really want and taste them. Something tells me my little hellcat won't react well to that just yet.

"Tomorrow at seven," I remind her tapping her lips with my finger as I draw my hand away.

"I guess I don't really have a choice, do I?" she smarts off, glaring at me, before she stalks off.

I watch her as she bends and slips seamlessly through the fence like a cat. I frown, knowing from my earlier inspection that fence is barbed wire. I'll have to remedy that immediately. I don't want her accidentally tearing her pretty skin on the barbs, though I'm sure she's got plenty of experience slipping through the fence if the practiced way she just flounced through it is any indication. Still, I won't risk her safety.

I continue to watch her retreating form until I see her nearing the little house in the distance.

I don't turn to walk back to my own house until she disappears behind the garage next door and out of my sight.

I've been wondering how I was going to approach her. I was thinking I was going to have to really stalk her to find a way to run into her again. I knew from the research I did as soon as I got to my new home that she was my neighbor, but finding her on my property had more than worked out to my advantage.

It's like we're fated to be and the universe is working to make it happen.

As if I need any more proof that she's meant to be mine.

CHAPTER THREE

Daisy

I'M a bundle of nerves all day. It's a good thing it doesn't take much focus for me to care for the plants at the nursery where I work because I keep tripping over the water hose and stumbling over my own two feet. I know it's because I'm nervous about tonight. I have no clue what to expect from this man I hardly know.

And, frankly, that terrifies me. I might not be afraid of snakes or bugs or coyotes. I've been baiting my own fishing hook since I was five years old. I'm a regular tomboy. Fearless. But the thought of dinner with one darkly alluring, mysterious man has me jumping at every turn.

Damn him.

I'm still fuming about how Nick coerced me into going out with him tonight. I realize that on some level I should be flattered that a man as hot as him even wants to go out with me, but I just can't get over the way he steamrolled me into it.

So what if he's gorgeous? The man's been rubbing me the wrong way from the moment I met him. Reprimanding me for saving an innocent animal. Ordering me around. Staring at me with his gorgeous eyes like he owns me or something.

I'll be damned if I let him get away with it.

I'm still in a pissy mood when I stalk into the house when I get home, letting the screen door slam shut behind me.

"What's got your panties all in a twist, Daisy Doo?" my dad asks me from where he's sitting with his feet propped up in his Lazy Boy recliner. He's still wearing his work clothes, so I can tell he just came in from where he works on the farm up the road. Mom will kill him if she sees him sitting on the furniture without changing out of his dirty clothes first.

I groan. "I have a date tonight."

I watch as my dad's brow furrows in confusion. "I

know I'm getting old, honey, but shouldn't you be happy about that? Not looking like you just swallowed a fly?"

"I'm fine, daddy," I tell him before going over to place a kiss on his forehead. "Just had a long day at work." It's not exactly a lie. My day had seemed overly long with me stressing all day about tonight.

"Is McAllister working you too hard?" Dad frowns. "You need me to have a talk with him?"

"No." The last thing I need is my dad telling my boss to cut me some slack. I'd never live it down. The guys who work at the nursery with me already tease me enough as it is and try to outdo me in everything.

"I'm fixing to go take a shower and get cleaned up. I suggest you do the same before Mom comes home and sees you like that." I raise an eyebrow at him, and he sighs, knowing I'm right.

I glance at the grandfather clock in the living room and wince when it begins to chime six times.

Crap. I've only got an hour until I have to endure whatever Nick has in store for me.

Daisy

I try to tell myself that I couldn't give a shit less what Nick thinks about how I look, that I'm not going to go out of my way to dress up for the man who gave me practically no choice in this matter, but I still find myself putting on a strapless little black dress that I've only ever worn once—to a dance in high school, no less. I just don't have very many fancy clothes. With not much occasion to wear them, why bother? When I'm not working at the nursery, I'm usually wandering around outside anyway. I hate being cooped up in the house, and I like to be comfortable.

The *only* reason I'm not stubbornly wearing something more casual is because I'd be mortified if Nick took me somewhere kind of fancy and I stood out like a sore thumb. Not that there are many fancy joints around here, but you never know.

I refuse to let him make a fool out of me. That's all. It has absolutely nothing to do with the way the dress clings to my curves or shows off my legs.

And the only reason I put on the barest hint of makeup is because it complements the dress. I'm not purposefully trying to make my eyes pop with the mascara that only makes my lashes look longer.

The one thing I absolutely do not bother with is my hair. I wear it long and loose and wild. I know I could straighten it and that would make it look sleek and beautiful, but I don't want him to think I've put too much effort into my appearance.

Because I haven't at all.

When I see it's about ten till seven, I walk downstairs, determined to go outside and meet Nick before he has a chance to come to the door. I don't want to go through the motions of introducing him to my parents when we absolutely will *not* be doing this ever again.

My annoyance instantly flares when I hear voices rising up to meet me as I walk down. I hear Mom and Dad talking, but they're not only talking to one another.

Damn him.

Nick's ass is lounging on our living room sofa like he owns the damn place while he smiles charmingly at my parents and tells them all about the software company he owns.

Wait. What? He *owns* a software company? It strikes me all over again how little I know about this man I'm going out with tonight, and if I wasn't afraid that he might actually make good on his threat to have me arrested for trespassing, I might actually high-tail it back upstairs to the safety of my room.

I consider doing it anyway, thinking that maybe a jail cell is preferable to the dangerously sexy man sitting in my parents' living room, but I've been spotted. Nick rises to stand as his eyes latch onto me where I stand on the second from last stair. His eyes sweep over my form appreciatively, and I feel my cheeks color under his open gaze in front of my parents.

He looks sinfully handsome in black slacks and a light grey button-up, his dark hair swept carelessly back from his face.

"Daisy, why didn't you tell us you met the man who bought Mr. McEwen's place?" Mom asks me, still smiling at Nick like he hangs the moon.

Even my dad seems smitten by him if the grin on his face is any indication, and I can't help wondering what Nick said to them before I came down that has them both beaming at him like so.

I don't answer Mom as I finish stepping down into the living room, thanking god that I can walk in my heels with how my legs are shaking. I've never been one for stilettos, and I've never been more thankful that I settled for kitten heels instead of the stilts of death other girls wear.

"I thought you said you'd be here at seven?" I say tightly through the smile I've plastered onto my face for the sake of my parents.

"Oh, I was in the neighborhood, so I thought I'd drop by a bit earlier to meet your parents," his eyes twinkle with his bit of wit.

"Punctuality is a value that can never be overrated," my dad chimes in while Mom's still swooning over the way Nick smiled as he said he wanted to meet them.

The bastard. He's turning my own parents to his side.

"You look beautiful," Nick murmurs to me as he comes to take my arm and lead me out of the door to the car that looks like it costs more than my parents' house. It's certainly not the rental he was driving yesterday, though that had been nice too. I wonder if he owns this vehicle, but then I firmly remind myself that I don't care.

"Have her home by eight!" my dad calls behind us, chuckling at his own joke.

"Oh, Merv," Even though I'm not looking back at them, I can just see Mom shoving Dad playfully. "She's an adult, for god's sake. Keep her all night if you want to, Nick!" Mom calls behind us.

My face turns scarlet with mortification as I turn back to glare at her, Nick's chuckle ringing in my ears. I swear. My mother is something else.

He opens the passenger-side door of his fancy little sports car, holding it open for me. He shuts it behind me when I get in and then walks around to the driver's side, a wide grin still plastered on his face as he somehow folds his huge body into the driver's seat.

"You ready?" he asks me while putting the car in gear.

"Does it matter?" I cross my arms in irritation.

He chuckles. "Well, I am," he says, "especially since I get to keep you all night if I want." He casts a teasing smirk my way.

"You most certainly do not," I hiss at him, my face turning red again.

He laughs outright as he pulls out of the driveway. "What? Your mother said I could."

"She's ridiculous," I fume, wanting to strangle her.

"I like her," he smiles at me, flashing his perfect set of white teeth over at me.

"Where are you taking me?" I change the subject.

"Ever been to Emilio's?" he asks me.

I know the place he's talking about. It's a five-star restaurant about two hours away from here in the city. I know some husbands take their wives there for anniversaries if they really want to splurge, but it certainly isn't the type of place a simple little country mouse like me has ever been to.

"No, but it's like two hours away. We can't go there," I protest.

"Who said we were?" He turns his wolfish grin at

me as he throws on his blinker even though there's no one behind us and turns into the long, winding driveway that leads back to the mansion that used to be Mr. McEwen's.

The mansion that is now his.

He pulls up to the front door and throws the car into park.

I look up at the stone exterior of the breathtaking home. It's rustic and contemporary all at the same time. I suddenly realize that I've never been inside it before. Before building it, Mr. McEwen lived in the modest home he built further up on his land. We passed it on the driveway out to the mansion. After his wife left him, he moved back into his previous home, and that's where Jake and I always visited him.

I wonder where he is now. I hope wherever he is he's happy. Or healing at least.

"If you just wanted me to meet you at your house, you could have told me, and I could have walked over," I tell Nick.

"That'd have been a pretty long hike dressed like that," he comments, his eyes sliding down my legs to my tiny heels.

I hate myself for blushing under his golden-eyed gaze.

"Why'd you ask me about Emilio's if we're not

going there?" I ask him as he opens the door and holds out a hand to help me out. I take his hand against my better judgement, not willing to risk falling, even if my heels are tiny.

It's the first time our palms have touched, and I feel a jolt throughout my entire system at the contact. I try, unsuccessfully, to hold in the gasp that escapes me.

His eyes darken as he pulls me closer to him, never releasing my hand.

Did he feel it too?

I swallow nervously and take a step back from him, though he refuses to release my hand.

"You'll see," he finally says by way of answering my question.

I let him lead me into his home, my curiosity getting the best of me.

I'm instantly awed by the wide foyer that show-cases a curving staircase that looks like something out of a Disney movie. The interior has the same theme as the exterior. Stone and clean lines that are somehow rustic and contemporary all at once. I can instantly see the perfect blending of masculine and feminine styles.

"Wow," I breathe.

"My thoughts exactly," Nick says lowly, and I glance at him to find him looking at me, studying my face.

I bite my lip nervously and look away, hating the way he makes me feel all bunched up inside.

"Come on, kitten," he chuckles as he moves closer to me, putting a hand on the small of my back to usher me forward. I try to ignore the way something melts within me when he calls me "kitten." All I can focus on is how tiny I feel with his huge hand spanning almost all the way across the small of my back as he leads me into the dining room.

Where there's a freaking chef waiting for us. Complete in a little white chef hat and everything. All he's missing is the little black mustache.

I glance at Nick quizzically as he pulls out the chair to the right of the one at the head of the table that's big enough to seat at least twenty people. He pushes the chair up under me as I sit, his hand grazing over my bare shoulder before he takes his own seat at the head of the table. The chef rattles off the name of each course, all of which is covered with a stainless steel dome, before he bows out and retreats back into the kitchen.

"Emilio's was the only acceptable restaurant I could find anywhere within a hundred mile radius of here, and I knew it was probably too far to drive on a first date, so I hired one of the chefs to come out and cook us a personal dinner," Nick offers by way of explanation as he pops the cork on a bottle of red wine and proceeds to pour us both a glass.

I blink at him, thinking of how incredibly thoughtful, if extravagant, that is before I suddenly process everything he said and hone in on one thing. "You say 'first date' like you think there will be others."

Nick lifts the dome to the first course to reveal soup and salad, and I follow suit with mine.

He seems entirely unconcerned with my comment as he answers, "Yes, there will be subsequent dates, kitten."

I can't hold back the snort of derision that leaves me. "Keep dreaming," I mutter.

He ignores my unladylike behavior, though, and continues talking like I didn't just have a rude outburst that my mother would be ashamed of.

I stab a bite of my salad and shovel it into my mouth, the tang of the perfectly balanced vinaigrette exploding on my tongue.

"How was your day?" he asks me politely. "Save any more turtles?"

I look up at him sharply to see the humor in his eyes.

"I'm glad I can be such a source of amusement for you," I say curtly.

He laughs outright at that, only stroking my ire

even more. I hate being teased. I absolutely hate it. I always have.

All throughout school I was teased for my red hair. Teased for having a temper to match. When I got older, the comments turned more savage with some of the meaner boys accusing me of having a "fire in the hole" even though I was so uptight I was considered a prude by most of the school. That's part of why I never could keep a boyfriend. I wouldn't put out.

I push back from the table and stand from my seat. I've had enough of his antics. "Did you just bring me here to make fun of me?" I cross my arms over my chest and glare down at him. Yeah, I'm pissed, but the thought that he only wants to poke fun at me stings, too.

He stops laughing, wisely sobering in light of my anger.

"Sit down, kitten," he orders me stoically, never rising from his seat.

"I think I should just go home. I'm sure this isn't going how you planned it would," I tell him honestly. Seriously, what is he doing with me here? I don't know how to act around him. He brings out the worst in me.

"Sit down," he repeats more firmly this time.

I harden my jaw at the order.

He finally looks up at me and sighs heavily. "If I

have to get up out of this chair and make you, you won't like the consequences. I promise you."

I glare at him some more, indignant at the way the man keeps bossing me around. He holds my gaze with his golden eyes, challenging me. I slowly lower myself back down to perch on the edge of the chair, his threat still ringing in the air between us. I don't know what the hell he'd do, but something tells me I don't want to find out.

"Eat," he commands, gesturing to my untouched dinner plate with his fork as he proceeds to take bites of his entree. I lift the dome of my own entree and take a cautious bite of the food.

Not because I'm obeying him. But because it smells delicious and I actually *am* hungry.

His eyes light with triumph at what he takes as my obedience.

I consider stabbing him with my fork.

Instead, I ask him, "So what do you do when you're not stalking women and threatening them over dinner?" I cock my head to the side innocently and smile sweetly at him in what's a blatant display of sarcasm.

"You're so beautiful when you smile at me like that," he murmurs. His statement catches me off guard, and my breath catches in my throat. His eyes never leave my face. He's staring at me in that intense way of his, and I have to fight to keep from squirming under his scrutiny.

I swallow the bite I'm chewing, not even tasting it. He gives me a breathtaking smile of his own like he knows exactly the effect he's having on me.

"I own a software development company." He says it likes it's no big deal, like it's a normal job.

"That sounds complicated," I comment back.

"It's demanding," he admits. "What about your job at the nursery?" he asks. "Do you enjoy it?"

"Should I even be surprised that you already know where I work, stalker?" I cock an eyebrow at him.

He grins devilishly. "One of the perks of owning an advanced software company. Plus, your dad was more than willing to volunteer the information while I was waiting for you to come down."

He frowns as he notices my untouched wine glass. "Do you not like the wine?"

"I don't know," I answer honestly. "I've never had wine before."

"Try it," he orders.

"I'm technically not old enough to drink," I point out to him.

His lips twist up into a smirk, "Since when are you averse to breaking the law, kitten?"

My eyes shoot daggers at him, but I take a tentative sip of the deep burgundy liquid anyway.

It's not the best thing I've ever tasted, but it's not the worst either.

He chuckles at the look on my face.

We continue to talk as we eat. Nick mostly asks me about the types of things I do at my job and if I've always lived here. What I like to do in my spare time. He keeps the conversation focused solely on me, and he pays such rapt attention to all my answers, his eyes never wavering from me like he's trying to memorize everything I say. It's both flattering and a bit unnerving. I'm not used to having such intense focus on me.

The food really is delicious, though, and Nick pours me another glass of wine after I finish the first one. I don't know if it's the wine or the conversation, but I begin to relax.

"So, are you going to give me a tour of the place?" I ask when we're finally done eating.

"Whatever you want, kitten," he stands, and I move to do likewise, but I wobble when I come to my feet, the room spinning just slightly.

"Easy there, hellcat," he's beside me in an instant, steadying me with his arms around my waist. I place my hands agains his chest, feeling how hard he is against my palms.

"Which is it? Hellcat or kitten?" I ask with a bit of a giggle, his arms still wrapped around me. I know why people drink now. I feel all floaty and happy.

His lips tip up as he looks down at me. "Both," he answers while trailing a finger down the side of my face. "You're adorable, like a sweet little kitten." His finger trails down my jawline and over my throat, "But you've got claws too, and sometimes you go feral on me."

"Animals only show their claws when they feel threatened," I whisper.

He places his thumb under my chin, the touch branding me where it touches my skin. "You have nothing to fear with me. I would never hurt you, kitten."

"You took my pond. It's my happy place," I say petulantly with a pout. I must be tipsy as hell to be admitting this to him. How I've always thought of it as my pond.

"You can visit it any time you want, kitten," he says softly. "I don't have a problem with that."

I look up at him gratefully. Maybe he's not so bad. Maybe we just got off on the wrong foot. God, he's so handsome.

He strokes his hand over my curls before he moves

that same hand around to cup the nape of my neck, tilting my head up to him.

His golden eyes are smoldering down at me, and even though I know it's coming and know I shouldn't let it happen, I don't stop it.

And nothing could have prepared me for the sensation of his full lips pressing against mine. Sure I've been kissed by boyfriends in the past, but those experimental touches didn't feel anything like this.

This must be what being kissed by a man feels like. His lips press firmly against mine, and then I feel his tongue stroking along my bottom lip, tasting me, before it runs along the seam of my lips, urging me to open to him.

When I slowly do, he wastes no time dominating my mouth, his tongue sliding in to take ownership of it. His tongue twines with mine as he sucks and nips on my bottom lip.

When I tentatively start to move my tongue against his, kissing him back, he groans, a deep guttural sound that rumbles in his chest. His hands fist in my hair and tilt my head even further back as he strokes his tongue in and out of my mouth in a way that even a virgin like me knows is reminiscent of the sexual act.

I feel flushed all over, and a strange wetness is pooling between my thighs. My core is thrumming in time with my heartbeat, and I'm gasping for breath by the time he finally pulls back enough to let me breathe.

"Daisy," he says my name softly as he strokes a thumb over my cheek.

"Wow," I say softly before I lean forward, dropping my head onto his chest, breathing in his scent. He smells so good—like sandalwood and something distinctly masculine that must just be him.

When I try to pull back from him to get my bearings about me, everything starts spinning. I shake my head, thinking that I must have had too much to drink for my first time, and then everything goes black.

CHAPTER FOUR

Nick

DAISY COLLAPSES IN MY ARMS, and I bend to scoop her up against me, cradling her to my chest. I'm mentally kicking myself for giving her more wine than she could handle. She's such a tiny thing. I should have guessed she might not be able to handle that much of such a strong vintage.

But I can't help loving the feeling of her tiny body cradled against me, the soft silkiness of her hair cascading down over my arms, the way her head turns into me as she sleeps softly.

I know I should probably lay her down on the

couch and leave her alone until she comes to, but instead I sit on the couch with her still cradled in my lap. I run my hands through her hair and study her angelic face.

Her milky white skin is marred only by precisely four freckles. One on the right side of her forehead, one to the left of her nose, one on the bottom of her left check, and one right along her hairline.

I stroke my hand along her hair, petting her like the docile little kitten she looks like sleeping peacefully in my arms. I trail my fingers over her neck and arms. While I might be tempted to touch all of her body, I don't. I'd never take advantage of her while she's sleeping.

I don't know how long I sit there and hold her, just enjoying the sweet vulnerability on her face as she slumbers. Something about the sweet serenity on her face when she's usually so feisty and sassy does something to me. To have such a little firecracker vulnerable and complacent in my arms brings out a surge of desire and protectiveness within me like I've never known.

It's probably an hour or more, and while I'd like nothing more than to just hold her like this all night, I'm not sure she'd appreciate waking up to find out she slept in my arms all night. She'd probably call me a creep. My lips quirk up at the thought.

And I need all the brownie points I can get with her if I want to win her the respectable way without kidnapping her.

It'd certainly be easier to just lock her up here and never let her leave.

But then I'm sure she'd hate me forever, and I don't want that.

So against all my desires, I finally begin to gently shake her awake. She hums a little sound of protest and burrows her head deeper into my chest. I feel a rush of male pride that she nuzzles closer to me even if it is subconcsiously.

"Daisy," I say her name softly as I continue to rouse her.

Her lips pout prettily, and I'm tempted to kiss them again. They look so luscious and pink.

Her lashes start to flutter, and then they snap open and zone in on my face. Reality comes crashing back down on her as she realizes where she is.

It bothers me way more than it should that her lips turn down into a frown when she recognizes me.

"Well, I can't say I've ever kissed a woman unconscious before," I joke, trying to lighten the mood and longing to see the fire flare in her eyes.

It works because her blue irises instantly ignite to become twin flames that I'd gladly burn in.

"I've never drank before," she protests, pushing against my chest to try to sit up.

I allow her to sit, though I keep her firmly planted on my lap with my hands on her waist, not willing to relinquish the contact just yet.

"How long was I out?" she asks, squirming on my lap. I have to bite back a groan at the friction she's unknowingly creating on my aroused cock.

"Long enough for me to know that you have exactly four freckles on your face." My voice comes out gruffer than I intend, thick with the sudden emotion clogging it. I've never felt this way about a woman before, like I could hold her all night and yearn to learn everything about her, like if she has freckles elsewhere.

She blushes and turns her face away from me, her long hair falling down to shield herself from my gaze. She gives a breathy laugh, "You counted my freckles?"

"Mmmhmmm," I hum against her hair, breathing in that honeysuckle scent of hers. "Makes me wonder if you have more." I trail my hand over her arm, testing the boundaries of what she'll allow. If I thought she'd be okay with it, I'd strip her down here and now and ravish her with everything in me, until she agrees that she'll always be mine and mine alone.

It would be so easy for me to become completely

consumed with her. I think she could quickly become an obsession.

Who am I kidding? She already is my obsession.

When I trail my hand down onto her bare leg, I feel her tremble in my arms as her breath hitches in her throat. The attraction pulsing between us is a living thing. I know she feels it too, but she's more resolute than I am because I feel her tiny hand cover mine to still my wanderings over the naked flesh of her thigh.

"I think I should go home now," she whispers.

I drop my forehead onto hers and look into her eyes with a groan, fighting to keep my body under control.

She holds my gaze boldly, either too innocent or too fearless to know the monster that lurks just beneath the surface and urges me to claim her in the most primal fashion.

I let out a breath that sounds shaky to my own ears as I force myself to pull back from her and move her off my lap to sit her on the couch next to me.

I need to add some space between us for what I need to tell her.

***

Daisy

"I don't want to kiss you goodnight, Daisy," Nick tells me, his voice sounding gruff.

I feel the embarrassment rising up within me. I know I'm no experienced kisser, but the confirmation that I'm horrible at it is humiliating.

The fact that I passed out right after it is humiliating.

I want to crawl into a hole and die.

But then I straighten my shoulders.

I quickly let my indignation take over my embarrassment. I didn't ask for any of this. I didn't ask for him to make me have dinner with him, and I certainly didn't ask for him to kiss me. On the contrary, I've fought him every step of the way and this right here is why. I know his type. Rich, spoiled, entitled, and way too sophisticated for a simple little girl like me. If he's disappointed, then it's his own damn fault. I will not let him make me feel stupid for something that I wanted no part of.

"I didn't ask you too," I retort, my response not quite having the venom that I intend. To my mortification, my voice comes out shaky, betraying some of the hurt at the thought that I'm such a disappointment to a man like him. And why wouldn't I be? He's cultured and refined, and I'm just a nobody from the sticks.

I start to stand, but he grabs my wrist in a firm grip

and then turns my head to face him with a hand on my chin. "I don't want to kiss you goodnight because it means this night is over," he tells me gently, looking into my eyes like he can see to those deepest parts of myself no one has ever seen.

"Oh," I say, not knowing what else to say.

He cracks a wry smile. "Plus, I'm afraid you'll go into a coma next time I kiss you."

My cheeks heat, and I pull away from him, standing and making my way over to the door. I'm leaving. I can walk back home.

He jumps up and laughs as he keeps stride with me. "Where are you going, kitten? I was just playing with you." He reaches out to grab my hand, but I yank it back from him.

I can't helping scoffing at him, "How do I know you didn't just put something in my drink to knock me out like that?"

I instantly know I've gone too far when his face darkens, his jaw line hardening. "You think I would drug you?" he asks me, his voice carefully controlled as he towers over me.

"I don't know," I lie, shrugging nonchalantly to try to hide my nervousness. "I don't really know you. And you did blackmail me into this dinner with you." True, I don't know him, but somehow I just know he wouldn't ever do something like that. Maybe I shouldn't have even insinuated it, but I hate being teased. The man pushes all my buttons and brings out my claws.

His nostrils flare, and I have to fight my instinct to flinch away from him.

"I may not always play fair," he says, his voice low with his barely contained fury, "but let me make one thing very clear. I would never drug a woman or take advantage of her."

I swallow at the intensity of his gaze and nod, licking my lips nervously. "I believe you," I tell him.

That seems to calm him somewhat because his jaw loosens slightly.

There's a moment of silence during which he just stares at me in that intense way of his. I can't sit still when he does it. I hate myself for it, but I fidget under his gaze like a shy schoolgirl, turning my feet in toward one another in a nervous habit.

I finally decide I have to break the silence since it's obvious he's not going to be the one to do it. "Thank you for the lovely meal," I tell him sincerely, "but I really should be getting home now."

He frowns down at me. "Is there no way I can convince you to stay longer?" he asks, taking a step closer to me.

I shake my head. "I really need to go."

He studies me a moment before he sighs and then moves to grab his car keys from the bowl he threw them in when we first walked into his home.

"I can walk home," I protest. "There's really no need for you—"

"Daisy," he places his hands on my shoulders as he says my name sternly in a tone that brooks no argument. "I'm driving you home. Do *not* fight me on this."

"I'm not a little girl—" I start to sass back, but Nick effectively silences me by grabbing both sides of my face in his huge hands and crashing his lips down onto mine.

This kiss is much more brutal than his first one was, as if he's pouring all the frustration he has with me out into it. His tongue swoops into my mouth, branding me and giving me nowhere to hide.

Despite myself, I melt against him, pressing my chest to his. His arms go around me triumphantly, pulling me flush against him. We're so close I can feel *that* hard, swollen part of him pressing against my stomach.

When he finally pulls back, he looks down at me, his golden eyes gleaming with the desire he makes no attempt to hide. "You're infuriatingly stubborn, you know that, kitten?" he says, his breath fanning over my lips. "It drives me fucking crazy."

"Nick," I whisper his name. That's all I get out before he kisses me again, gently this time. I don't know what I was going to say anyway. He peppers little kisses all over my face before he runs his nose along the side of mine in a move that's so tender it thaws something inside of me.

"You're going to be mine. You know that, don't you?" he whispers the words right into my ear.

I open my mouth on an instinctive protest, but he puts a finger to my lips, shushing me.

He already knows what's on the tip of my tongue, and he doesn't want to hear it.

"Let's take you home before I lose every ounce of my control," he finally says.

The thought that little ole' me could cause such a put-together man like Nick to lose control makes my stomach do a little flip-flop.

I don't know what to say, so for once I keep my mouth shut. I feel his eyes on me frequently on the short ride home, watching me like a panther ready to pounce on its prey.

Like a true Southern gentleman, he comes around and opens the car door, walking me up to the front door.

He cups my face with his hand, running his thumb over my cheek tenderly. "This isn't over, kitten," he promises me before he leans down and kisses me goodnight, a brief peck of his lips against mine.

I still don't say anything. I just turn to enter the house, my legs oddly wobbly feeling. He waits until I'm safely inside with the door latched before he turns to walk back to his car and drive back to his place.

I'm thankful my parents are both already in bed. I don't think I could handle my mother's meddling right now or my dad's teasing.

I go upstairs to my room and put on a big T-shirt to sleep in before I curl up in bed. The phone I left on my nightstand buzzes, and I pick it up, wondering who'd be texting me at this time of night.

Good night, kitten.

I haven't given Nick my phone number, but I'm completely unsurprised he has it. What's finding out a phone number to a tech genius like him?

I put my phone down without texting him back.

The man has my head spinning so that I don't know what to think.

As I drift off to sleep, though, the last thing I see are the two golden orbs of his eyes looking down at me like he wants to devour me.

CHAPTER FIVE

Daisy

ALTHOUGH I DON'T HAVE to work, I wake up early anyway. I've always been an early riser. Daddy says I've always gotten up with the chickens, and I guess that's true.

I'm sitting outside on our porch swing sipping my coffee when Jake's truck pulls up into the driveway.

He hops out of his truck and pulls a couple of fishing poles out of the bed before sauntering over to where I sit on the front porch.

I forgot all about us going fishing this morning.

"What? No coffee for me?" he asks as he leans the

fishing poles against the picket fence and bounds up the porch step to where I'm sitting.

I laugh. "Yeah, let me just go get us a thermos to go."

Jake takes a seat on the swing to wait for me as I creep into the house and pour the rest of the pot of coffee into a thermos before readying another pot for Mom and Dad for when they wake up. I grab a sticky note and write "Just push button on it" before slapping it onto the coffee pot where I know they'll see it.

The sun is barely starting to peek through on the horizon when I walk back outside. I hold the thermos while Jake carries the fishing poles and a tiny tub of crawlers.

We make our way over to the barbed wire fence and pause when there's a gate in the barbed wire. It actually looks rather ridiculous. There are two metal posts on other side of the gate. They connect to the barbed wire and serve as the structure for the shiny new black metal fence to hang on.

"Huh, what do you make of that?" Jake asks, walking up to it and swinging the gate open.

I know exactly what to make of it. Nick had a gate put up. Though I have my suspicions why, I don't say anything to Jake about it. I certainly don't tell Jake about the forced date I had with Nick just last night. I don't know if he'd tease me or be overly concerned, and I don't want to deal with either reaction right now when I'm still not entirely sure of what to make of all of it myself.

"I guess the new owner put it up," I say evasively.

"McEwen finally sold the place?" Jake asks me, his brows raising as we walk over to the pond and set to baiting our hooks.

"Yep," I say, adding nothing else, not letting on that I've met the man and that he's the most handsome, pushy, devilish man I've ever met.

"You think he'll mind us fishing here?" Jake frowns, just now realizing that we might have lost our favorite fishing hole.

"Yes, he *will* mind you trespassing on his property," a dark voice speaks from behind us.

My heart leaps up into my throat, and I turn to find Nick towering over us. Jake is pretty tall himself, but Nick has got an extra inch on him. He's sweaty, his black T-shirt clinging to his form. He's wearing workout shorts, and even his hair is glistening with beads of moisture. It's obvious he's been out for a morning jog across his property.

I've never been the kind of girl to find sweat on a man sexy, but damn if Nick doesn't look fine as hell with it glistening on his toned muscles.

"Hey, man," Jake holds his hands up, making it clear we meant no offense, "we didn't know. We've been fishing here since we were little kids. The previous owner never had a problem with it."

Nick's eyes are hard as they stare at Jake, sizing him up.

I tear my eyes from Nick's bulging biceps as he fists his hands and cross my arms over my chest, glaring at him. "I thought you said you didn't mind me coming here?"

I see Jake's head swivel to me in surprise. "Wait, you know this dude?"

Nick's eyes bore down into mine before they flick back to Jake. "Yes," he tells Jake smugly, "I'd say she does since we're dating."

My mouth drops open in shock. "Nick..." I begin, but he comes and wraps an arm around my back, pulling me to his side and away from Jake.

"You have exactly three minutes to get off my property," he tells Jake frankly.

Jake's eyes widen and flash to me with a hint of hurt. "Yeah, man, sure. Sorry," he tells Nick.

"Jake..." I begin, hating the hurt that I see in my best friend's eyes.

"It's okay, Daisy," he tells me, gathering up the fishing poles we never even got to cast into the water.

"We'll talk later, okay?" His eyes flick back to Nick, and then he ducks his head and hurries off, no doubt wanting to avoid further angering Nick.

I finally get my wits about me enough to pull myself away from Nick. I turn and spin to stare at him with my hands on my hips. "Just what the hell was that? You told me you didn't mind me coming here. If you didn't want me to, all you had to do was say so."

"I told you *you* could come here—not your fucking boyfriend," he growls, his golden eyes blazing.

I stare at him, and then I can't help it. I start laughing.

The thought of Jake and me being together...

Nick's brows furrow, and his expression looks thunderous.

"That's what this is about?" I finally manage to gasp out. "You think Jake is my boyfriend?"

Nick's jaw tightens.

"Not like it's any of your business," I tell him, "but Jake is not my boyfriend. He's more like a big brother to me."

"He wants to fuck you," Nick says resolutely, "and, yeah, it is my business. You're mine, so that makes you my business."

My eyebrows raise up to my hairline and my breath catches. "Yours?" I stare at him like he's sprouted another head before I shake my head incredulously, "I don't know where you get off thinking that."

He turns on the smolder, looking at me darkly as he takes a step toward me.

"What do you think this is, kitten?" he asks me softly, seductively, dangerously.

My heart begins to race, and all I can think about is how I need to put distance between us even as I half long for the touch of his fingers on my skin. How fucking confusing is that?

I take a step back from him when he takes another step forward. "What *what* is?" I ask him, unable to stop my blood from thrumming in my veins the closer he gets to me.

"This," he motions between us. "I know you feel it too. I can see you trembling every time I get close to you. I felt you soften in my arms last night every time I kissed you."

I feel my face heat at the reminder and wet my lips. His eyes dart down to them, and he licks his own as he zones in on them.

Despite me taking steps back, his steps are longer than mine, and he closes the distance between us, stilling me from retreating further by placing his hands on my waist.

He lowers his head until his lips are right beside my ear before he says, "Don't run from me, Daisy."

I don't have time to respond before he kisses me, deeply, passionately, one hand holding me by the nape of the neck, the other still firm on my waist.

He kisses me artfully, stealing my breath away, and I see he's right. I'm trembling all over by the time he pulls back just enough to allow me to breathe.

"Have dinner with me again tonight," his whispers right against my lips.

He doesn't ask. It's a command. Like he owns me. Which he apparently thinks he does, I'm quickly reminded. I purse my lips at his audacity and shake my head.

He narrows his eyes at me. "Don't make me blackmail you again because you know I will."

I look up into his eyes and realize with irritation that he's telling the truth. He's not above playing dirty to get his way.

It infuriates me. "You're despicable," I fume before turning on my heel and stalking away from him.

He just laughs behind me before calling out, "I'll come for you at seven."

I flip him off without even turning to look back at him.

He only laughs louder.

Damn him.

Daisy

I'm glad it's Saturday and I don't have to work today because I'm so mad I know I'd be distracted and wouldn't be worth a shit on the job.

I don't know who Nick thinks he is. He just rolls into town in his super fancy car and thinks he can just snap his fingers and take over my life. He's been bossy and domineering from the moment we met, and now he's declaring that I'm his like I'm a possession to be owned.

Never mind that I feel a flutter in my tummy at the possessive way he says the words and the way his eyes look at me when he says them—like I'm the most important thing in his world or something.

Maybe my body does melt for him, but that doesn't excuse the fact that the man bulldozes over me and never stops to ask me what I want. He blackmails and commands to get what he wants.

Entitled, spoiled, rich prick.

I'm probably another fun conquest in a long line of women.

Well, I'm done caving to his demands. I'm not some little pushover who swoons for a pretty face and gives him whatever he wants.

I stalk into the house and pour myself a glass of some of Mama's fresh lemonade. Even though it's not even noon yet, the humidity is high today, so it's already hot and sticky outside. Nothing is quite as refreshing as a glass of fresh-squeezed lemonade on a hot day. Normally I'd go swimming in the pond on a day like today, but I'll be damned if I willingly go anywhere near Nick or his goddamned land.

"Oh, hey, there, honey," Mom says as she walks into the kitchen, beaming at me. She and Dad have the weekends off, and I'm glad. They both work so hard. They deserve to at least have the weekends off.

"How did last night go?" she asks me with a sly grin. "I didn't hear you come home."

I roll my eyes at her. "I came home, Mom."

Her face seems to fall somewhat, and I can't help thinking that this is all backwards. Shouldn't my parents be berating me for staying out all night? Not encouraging me to do so? Nevermind that I'm eighteen and can technically stay out as late as I want. Living under their house with their rules, shouldn't they still be encouraging a curfew?

Mom crosses her arms over her chest and gives me

an assessing look, "You didn't answer my question. How did it go?"

I shrug, and Mom sighs dramatically.

"What?" I ask her defensively as I place my glass of lemonade on the counter.

"Daisy Ann," she inserts my middle name, letting me know that she means business with what she's fixing to say. "You've got to give someone a chance, honey. You push away every man who's ever tried to date you."

"I do not," I scoff.

She nods her head. "Yes, you do. What about Arnold?"

I give a sarcastic laugh. "He's my boss's son, Mom. That was hardly appropriate. Plus, I'm just not interested in him that way."

Mom nods her head and holds up a finger. "Then, what about Pastor Don's son? He's been smitten with you since you were twelve."

I wrinkle my nose up in distaste. Jason isn't a bad-looking guy, but he just *so* isn't the type of guy for me.

Mom keeps holding up fingers, ticking off the names of guys who've wanted to date me. I actually tried with some of them, but in the end, I always broke it off.

"Okay, okay," I hold up my hand to stop her. "I get

it, Mom. You think I'm a commitment-phobe or something."

She sighs again and looks at me like she doesn't know what to do with me. "All I'm saying, honey, is that you need to give someone a chance. You could do a lot worse than Nick Amorini. Not only is he rich, but he seems like a respectable man. You could have a good life with him."

Nick Amorini. I didn't even known his last name until now. It strikes me as odd that my parents know his surname before I do.

Something about the name sounds familiar, though I can't put my finger on it.

"Gee, Mom. Keep it up, and I'll think you just want to marry me off to get me out of the house," I try to deflect her concern with a joke.

She frowns. "You know that's not it at all. I just want you to be happy, honey."

I grab an apple from the fruit bowl sitting on the counter and take a bite out of it before I give her a kiss on the cheek and turn to bound up the stairs to my room. "I am happy, Mom," I tell her as I go.

But I hear her sigh behind me. Mom is from that generation that thinks a girl my age needs to be settling down and getting married already. Almost everyone my age around here is already married or well on their way to it. No matter that I'm barely legal. Some of those old South ways have still stuck here in the sticks. Some of the girls I went to school with were actually barefoot and pregnant at sixteen.

Stuff like that was never for me. I like my freedom, thank you very much. When you get married, suddenly you have to be an adult, popping out kids and taking care of the house. There'd be no more fishing in the mornings with Jake or climbing trees or lazing the day away reading books under the dogwood tree.

The truth is I've never been ready to give up my tomboy ways for all that domesticity.

I like doing what I want when I want. I like to think I'm an independent woman.

That's why there's no way I'm going to let Nick Amorini plow his way into my life and start ordering me around like he owns me.

When I get upstairs to my room, I grab my phone and fall down onto my bed, typing his name into the search bar.

I halfway don't expect anything to pop up. That's why my eyes about pop out of my head when I see the sheer volume of search results I'm hit with at a search of Nick's name.

Software tech billionaire. One of Boston's most

eligible bachelors. His parents died in a car crash when he was just a teen. My heart aches for him there. I can't imagine what I'd do without my mama and daddy.

I click over to the image search and feel my stomach plummet when there's picture after picture of him on the arm of beautiful women. He's never shown with the same woman twice. And the women he's pictured with are beautiful. Like drop dead gorgeous model types. They're tall and curvy with generous breasts. Blonde bombshells and brunette babes. The type of women who put my skinny little frame and freckled little redheaded self to shame.

As if I needed any more proof that my inclinations were right all along.

I'm just a little backwoods country mouse who's probably only so intriguing to him because of the chase of something different. Once he has me, he'll toss me to the side like all the rest.

But that won't happen because he'll never have me. I refuse to be another conquest for a rich playboy.

CHAPTER SIX

Nick

I'M EARLY AGAIN to pick up Daisy. I'm surprised I was able to wait as long as I did.

I should have just taken her back to my house this morning after I'd caught her by the pond with that boy. My jaw clenches again at the thought of her with him. She might protest that they're just friends, but a man knows when another man wants what's his, and that boy wants her whether he's made a move on her or not. Little does he know he'll have her over my dead body. Daisy is *mine*. As irrational as it is, she's been mine since the moment I first saw her stopping traffic to save a goddamned turtle.

Her grandmother's old Buick is parked in their driveway when I pull up. Yeah, I did my homework on her entire family. It doesn't bother me at all to see the Cunninghams have company. I'll have to meet her entire family one day anyway when I finally convince Daisy to be mine in every way. Might as well ingratiate myself to all of them as soon as possible.

I kill the engine to my Maserati and walk cooly up the steps to their quaint little cottage-style home.

Daisy's mom looks thrilled to see me again if her beaming smile is any indication, and her dad seems jovial as well. The grandmother I've never met is eyeing me suspiciously. Guess the verdict is still out on me there. No matter. If she's important to Daisy, I'm determined to win her over too.

"Who's this young pup?" the old woman asks from where she sits in a glider chair rocking gently back and forth, her shrewd eyes never leaving me.

Before I can introduce myself, Daisy's dad answers, "This is Nick Amorini, the man who bought old Mr. McEwen's place. I take it you're here for Daisy?" The man directs that last question at me.

"Yes, sir," I answer him before walking over to the old woman and holding out a hand for her to shake. I know her type already, bred in the age of manners and chivalry.

She takes it in a grip that's surprisingly firm for her fragile frame. "What're your intentions with our Daisy?" she cuts right to the chase.

I hold her eyes and don't hesitate with my answer. "I want to marry her."

I realize it might be fast, but it's true. That's the end goal here. I want Daisy completely tied to me. I want her to be mine. Forever.

The old woman never blinks. She just stares at me as if assessing the truthfulness of my answer, and then she cackles. "I like you, young man."

I feel a genuine grin split my face at having met the approval of the matriarch of the family. I can see Daisy's mom beaming at me from the corner of my eye.

"Let me just see if Daisy's ready," Mrs. Cunningham tells me before disappearing upstairs where Daisy's room must be.

Mr. Cunningham makes small talk with me until his wife comes back down the stairs. She's frowning, but she tries to cover it with an apologetic smile, "Daisy's not upstairs. I'm sure she didn't forget your plans tonight, but sometimes she looses track of time when she's roaming about out on the land."

I know better, though. This was intentional. Daisy

is sending me a message that she's not going to just do whatever I say. She's still angry at me. Unfortunately for her, her defiance only makes my dick hard. I feel a smile twitch at the corners of my lips.

"She's probably got her nose stuck in a book somewhere," Mr. Cunningham grunts.

Daisy's grandmother is watching me like a hawk, and I have a feeling her eyes miss nothing. In fact, I bet she knows her tenacious granddaughter better than any of them and has already figured out exactly what's going on. "Try the woods out back, young man."

"Thank you, ma'am," I nod at her. "I'll do that, if you don't mind," I glance at Daisy's father for permission to tramp about on his land.

He motions me on with a wave of his hand.

I can already feel my blood thrumming with the thrill of the chase.

Daisy

I almost fall off the tree limb I'm perched on when I hear tromping footsteps below me and look down to see Nick's darkly alluring form making his way through the woods.

His dark hair is falling haphazardly over his face in that carelessly fashionable way, and he's wearing his customary dark slacks and a gray button-up.

He looks sinfully handsome—sinfully being the operative word.

His eyes are scanning all around. He's looking for something.

Someone.

Me.

I hold my breath as I stare down at him, but it's like there's a magnetic pull connecting us because his head tips up and his eyes come up to meet mine, piercing me with their intensity despite the distance between us.

He swears under his breath before calling up to me, "What the fuck are you doing up there? You could break your goddamned neck."

I roll my eyes at him. I've been climbing trees almost since I could walk. I'll be fine. I don't tell him that, though. Instead I simply call down to him smugly, "You do realize you're trespassing on our land?"

His face breaks into a wolfish smile as he shakes his head. "I have your father's permission to be here, little jailbird."

I scowl down at him, pissed that I don't finally have something to lord over his head like he does me.

He just throws his head back and laughs. "Come down here, Daisy, and let's talk."

I settle my back against the tree trunk and smile down at him saucily. "I'm just fine where I am, thanks."

He shakes his head and curses again. Good. Hopefully, I'll piss him off enough he'll go away.

My eyes widen in consternation when he comes over to the tree and swings himself up on the first branch, hauling his big body up in a fluid movement.

"What the hell are you doing?" I ask him as he climbs resolutely up to where I am.

Damn it. I'd thought I was safe from him up here, but I've actually effectively treed myself. I have nowhere to run to get away from him. In my defense, I hand't counted on a city boy like him being able to climb a tree.

He doesn't answer me until he's standing on the branch right below me. The height of it puts his face level with mine, and I can't even lean back to escape his proximity without risking falling from the tree.

"You're the most infuriating woman I've ever met," he tells me, his breath fanning over my lips.

"So you've said," I snap back. "So why bother?"

His golden eyes rove over my face before they settle back on my lips. "Fuck if I know," he growls before he wraps a hand around my back and holds me still as his lips crash onto mine.

I cling to him as he devours me, partly because I can't help melting into his possessive kisses and partly because I don't want to topple out of the tree.

"Come down," he orders me when he finally pulls back just enough to allow me room to breathe.

I nod my agreement and then follow him as he climbs back down the tree. I have to come down sometime anyway, right?

My feet don't even get to touch the ground. He's waiting for me at the bottom of the tree, and as soon as I start to swing myself down from the last branch, he puts his shoulder into my stomach and flings me over his shoulder.

"Nick!" I scream, beating my hands on his back. It's no use, though. His back is like a hard slab of marble, and he doesn't even flinch under the assault. "Put me the fuck down!"

"Don't curse," he reprimands me, and that only serves to piss me off even more.

"Fuck! Shit! Fuck! Shit!" I scream, kicking my legs as he stalks resolutely through the woods, never slowing his stride.

Suddenly, I feel a hard swat as his palm connects with my ass. It stings even through my jean shorts.

I gasp, "What the *fuck* do you think you're doing?" I'm outraged and start to wiggle even more. "Put. Me. Down!"

"That's another one," he grunts, his hand coming down to smack my ass again, causing another sting to spread across my cheek. "One for each time you've cursed," he says, his hand coming down on my ass three more times.

I can't believe he's spanking me. It's fucking humiliating.

I'm seething.

"You going to watch that pretty mouth of yours? I guaran-fucking-tee I have a better way to fill it with filth if that's what you're determined to do," he comments dryly.

He finally stops walking and pulls me from his shoulder, sliding me down his front as he does so until my feet touch the ground. He doesn't release his hands from where he holds my hips against him, and I can feel his arousal through his pants.

I glare up at him defiantly. My cheeks are flaming at both his dirty innuendo and the aftermath of the spanking. He just looks down at me stoically.

"Oh, so you can cuss and I can't? Hypocrite much?" I snark up at him.

He throws his head back and laughs.

"How dare you strike me!" I hiss at him.

He shakes his head, his golden eyes darkening. "Not strike. Spank. Discipline. There's a difference."

"I don't need discipline from you," I spit at him. "You're not my daddy."

"On the contrary," he says, his eyes burning into mine, "I'm the only daddy you're ever going to have again."

He cranes his head down until his lips are so close to mine I can feel them dancing along mine as he whispers, "And you loved every fucking minute of it."

"You're insane," I tell him.

He smirks against my lips before he takes them in a rough kiss. I feel his fingers touching me through my shorts, and it's like electricity zings right between my legs. He groans into my mouth, a rumble that goes straight to my core, and then I feel his fingers sliding up under my shorts, pushing them and my panties to the side in one swift motion.

Those fingers stroke over my most intimate of places, and then he pulls his hand back from my shorts, holding it up with a triumphant smirk on his face.

"Told you you liked it. You're fucking soaked for me." His fingers are glistening with my juices, and my face heats at his words.

My eyes widen when he puts those same fingers in

his mouth and tastes me, never break eye contact with me as he does so.

It's so dirty and the look in his eyes is so dark and lustful that I can't stop myself from trembling. There's a pulsing thrum between my legs, and my breath catches in my throat.

"You taste like honey," he tells me before he captures my lips in a deep kiss, thrusting his tongue into my mouth, making me taste myself. It's the most erotic thing that's ever happened to me.

I feel my legs buckling and throw my arms around him, clinging to him to keep from falling to the ground.

He holds me up with one hand tight against my waist and another secured at my neck while he kisses me until I can't think straight.

Before I even know what's happening, he's lowered me to lay on a blanket that was already spread out on the ground, his lips never leaving mine as he continues to kiss me the entire way down.

When I'm laying flat on my back, his kisses move from my mouth to trail over my jaw and neck. I feel his hand skimming up under my tank top to touch the bare skin of my stomach. Despite myself, I arch up into his touch.

"Yes, kitten," he whispers against my skin as his lips move lower onto my collarbone.

He kisses me worshipfully, licking and nipping at every inch of skin he can find while his hand continues to travel upward until I feel it slip beneath the cup of my bra.

I whimper at the contact as he rolls a nipple between his thumb and forefinger, his lips kissing the swell of my breasts now.

I can't stop the cry that escapes me when he encloses the hard bud in his hot mouth, his tongue flicking over it tantalizingly.

It's not long before his head starts kissing its way over my stomach, causing my tiny abs to quiver beneath his lips.

"You're everything," he whispers against my stomach as his fingers deftly undo the buttons of my shorts.

"So fucking beautiful," he continues as he pulls them and my panties from my body in one swift move.

I should probably stop him. I said I wasn't going to be just another notch on his belt. I don't want to be just another one in his long slew of women.

But I can't make my mouth form the words. Not when his lips are branding me with fire with every wet kiss across my skin.

His lips are traveling lower now, over my pelvis and to my inner thighs.

I feel his breath fanning over my pussy, and I try to close my legs, but he won't let me. He holds my legs open with his hands as he looks down at the part of me no one has ever seen before.

"Nick, no one has ever..." I begin, but then I trail off, too embarrassed to tell him I'm a virgin.

He stills and looks up at me, his golden eyes gleaming amber as he confirms, "No one has ever kissed you here before, Daisy?"

I bite my lip nervously and shake my head.

A choked noise escapes him, and his breathing becomes heavier. I feel his hands tighten on my thighs where he holds me open. "Has anyone ever been inside you before?" he croaks out.

I shake my head again, pulling against him and trying to crawl away. "I'm sorry," I apologize for my inexperience, embarrassed beyond words.

He gives a hoarse laugh, "Sorry? I should be thanking you. Now I don't have to kill anyone."

Before I can say anything else his mouth is on me, licking all along my slit up to my clit.

I jump at the sensation of his tongue sliding over my swollen nub, but he holds me still, not letting me pull away.

"Don't ever run from me, remember?" he chides

me before doing another one of his torturously long licks.

"You have the prettiest fucking pussy I've ever seen, kitten," he tells me in between licks.

Suddenly, he plunges his tongue into me, fucking it in and out of my wet folds. I gasp, my hands shooting down to fist in his hair. He's circling my clit with the pad of his thumb while he continues to tongue-fuck me. I feel pressure building within me and can't stop the whimpers and moans that escape me.

"That's it, baby," he encourages me as he continues his rhythm.

I don't know what my body's chasing, but it's something that I desperately need in this moment.

He increases the speed with which he's circling my clit and prods my opening with his finger. "Come for me, kitten," he demands, and just like that, my body obeys and convulses into my first mind-blowing orgasm.

Nick

Her pussy contracts around my finger where I've barely inserted it into her. I can feel her muscles gripping and rippling around it, and I feel the cum shooting up the stalk of my dick as I imagine it sheathed in her depths as she falls apart like this.

To my utter amazement, I feel my release burst from my tip, making a sticky mess in my boxers. I groan as I feel my fluids ripping from me.

"Goddamn, baby," I rasp as I smash my hips into hers and grind myself against her as the rest of my cum pumps from my body, "You made me fucking come without even touching you."

I can honestly say I've never in my whole fucking life come in my pants just from eating a chick out. But that's what Daisy does to me. I lose all fucking control around her, and I can only imagine what it'll be like when I get inside her. Two fucking pumps and I'll probably be done.

I look down at her flushed face. Her eyes are still closed as she practically purrs in the afterglow of the orgasm I gave her. It's probably for the best I shot my first preliminary load in my pants. I'm still hard as a rock. Maybe now I can fuck her without exploding as soon as I slide into what I already know will be the gates of heaven.

Fucking hell, when she admitted she was a virgin... Christ, I knew she was mine, but the thought that she'll be totally *mine* in every way. No other man will ever taste the sweet nectar of her cunt. No other man will ever fill her the way I will.

I kiss her lips gently, coaxing her back to the present. I want to look into her beautiful blue eyes when I first slip inside her and make us one person.

Still drunk on her afterglow, she slides her thin arms around my neck and kisses me back languidly. Her tongue twining with mine is the sweetest thing I've ever experienced.

I still can't believe she apologized for her inexperience. Hell, it's the best gift I've ever received. I don't want a practiced body underneath mine. I want *her*. Just as she is. Sweet and innocent and fiery and sassy.

While still kissing her lips, I undo the buttons of my slacks and pull myself from my boxers, not bothering to completely undress myself. Maybe I'm not playing fair again, but I don't want to give her mind a chance to catch up with her and fuck us out of this. Her body wants me. Her *soul* wants me. Whether she realizes it or not, this is how we're meant to be.

Still keeping her drunk on kisses, I line myself up at her entrance. Despite how wet she is, I can still feel how tight she is against my tip.

My body aches as I hold back the urge to plunge within her in one thrust. Instead, I plunge my tongue deeper into her mouth as I press slowly into her, slipping just the head of my cock inside her tight channel.

She cries out in my mouth, her body tensing beneath me at the intrusion.

I slip a hand between us and begin to work her clit in smooth circles again.

She manages to tear her lips from mine and looks up at me with wild eyes. "Nick," she pleads my name, her tiny hands gripping my biceps.

"I've got you kitten," I tell her, stroking my hand over her hair, petting her, soothing her.

She whimpers as I press another inch into her. I feel the head of my shaft hitting her hymen, and I know the point of no return is upon us. I can either drag it out, pushing in slowly, which will probably be more painful for her considering my length and girth, or I can make the pain swift and tear through swiftly.

My balls are already churning, so I force myself to sit still for a moment as I drop kisses all over her face. "Sweet girl, beautiful girl," I can't stop raining praises on her. She's the most gorgeous sight I've ever seen with her red curls splayed out all around the blanket, her lips red and swollen from my kisses, her eyes blue pools looking up at me trustingly and hesitantly.

I hate to hurt her, but I keep my eyes trained on hers as I pull back slightly and without any warning plunge the rest of the way into her. I'll never forget the blue of her eyes as I take her for my own the first time.

She screams, her back arching up with the pain, but I capture her cries with my lips, swallowing them as I kiss her back into submission.

Her sweet cunt is squeezing me like a vice. She's so fucking tight I feel like I'm going to pop already. I feel sweat starting to bead across my brow, and every muscle in my body is wound up tight with the effort I'm making to stay still to give her time to adjust to me.

Mine! my mind chants at me. I'm inside her now, connected to her in a way no one else will ever be.

"Tell me I can move now, Daisy," I beg against her lips. I know it's ironic as hell. I haven't asked her permission for a damn thing since I've met her. I've railroaded her at every turn, but I want to know she wants this too. I don't ever want her to be able to deny this moment.

"Yes," she moans as she shifts her hips up to me, gasping when I slide inside her, creating a friction in a place where she's never felt it before.

Thank God she said yes because that little moan is what does it. The thread I'm hanging by snaps, and I can't stop myself from stroking in and out of her heat. I try to go slow with long, sensuous strokes, both to heighten her pleasure and prolong my own, but the beast takes over, and within minutes, I'm ramming into her as deep as I can get.

I grab her arms and legs and wrap them around me. "Hold onto me, baby," I rasp at her before I plummet into her, pounding her as her cries echo around us, driving me onward.

"Mine!" I tell her in between thrusts. "Tell me you're mine, Daisy."

I know it's wrong to try to elicit promises from her in the heat of the moment, but I don't care. The need is too great, and I'm half-crazed with my lust. I can't think straight. All I can do is feel her. See her. My entire world laid out before me.

I ram into her hard, prompting her again. "Say it," I demand.

"Yours!" she finally screams as the first ripples of pleasure grip her. I can feel her pussy quivering around me.

"Who's?" I prompt her again, stabbing her with shallow thrusts until she gives me what I want.

She sobs with need. She's right there ready to tip over the precipice, but I won't let her until she seals her fate to mine.

"What's my fucking name?" I growl out. I want her to know exactly who the fuck is fucking her, who she belongs to until the end of time now. I'm holding back, but my own control is slipping.

"Nick!" she shouts. I pump as deep as I can into her, dragging my dick along her g-spot. She screams in pleasure. I feel her pussy quake as she falls apart in the throes of another orgasm.

"Damn right," I grunt out. I'm right there with her.

My balls are tight. I feel them drawing up into me, and I look down into her eyes, wanting to memorize the look in them as I release myself into her for the first time, making her as mine forever.

I roar out her name as my release tears through me in the most blindingly intense orgasm of my life. My cocks swells as it dumps spurt after spurt of sperm into her. I don't think I've ever come so much, especially after already coming before I ever got inside her.

I fall onto the blanket next to her, knowing that I'm too big to put the full force of my weight on her. I drag her limp form into my arms and cradle her against my chest while I catch my breath.

She feels so good, so *right*, in my arms.

I'm never letting her leave them.

CHAPTER SEVEN

Daisy

I'M STILL LAYING TUCKED up against Nick's chest when I finally start to come back down to earth after the mind-numbing orgasms he just put my body through.

Yeah, there was pain like I'd always heard there would be with a first time, but the pleasure...

I never knew it could be like that.

I see the glisten of water out of the corner of my eye and turn my head to see we're laying right next to the pond.

I try to pull out of Nick's arms to sit up and fix my

state of undress. My tank top and bra are still pulled up to reveal my breasts. My panties and shorts are otherwise discarded.

One glance at Nick shows that he somehow managed to retain all of his clothing. His shirt is still on, and he's already tucked mostly away in his pants. All he has to do is zip up.

Apparently I'm the only one who had to be more exposed.

I notice we're laying on a blanket, which indicates that Nick had something planned here.

I stiffen in his arms and try to pull away again, but he holds me fast.

"Where do you think you're going, kitten?" he asks me lazily. I feel him plant a kiss on the top of my forehead.

"Did you have this planned?" I ask him, trying to keep my voice even.

He tips my head up to him with a finger under my chin. He looks straight into my eyes as he tells me, "This specifically? No. If you're referring to the blanket, I had it ready to wine and dine you on a picnic."

"A picnic?" I question, my heart softening within me. A picnic by the water has always been my idea of the perfect date.

He smiles that devastating smile of his at me, like he can see my pleasure at the thought.

"Something told me a picnic by your pond would be the most romantic gesture I could make with you."

He reaches out and tucks a curl behind my ear, but it's to no avail because it just springs free again.

I can only imagine the mess my hair must look. But then again when is my wild mane not a mess?

"It's your pond now," I remind him softly.

He shakes his head. "It's ours now."

I blush as his meaning becomes clear. He's referring to the fact that it'll always be *our* place now. The place where he took my virginity. The place where he claimed me and made me his.

"I don't regret the turn of events," he tells me seriously.

"Don't you either, Daisy," he warns me. "This was how it was always going to end anyway. With you in my arms."

For once, I don't argue. I don't let myself get offended by his possessive statements. Instead, I just bask in the feeling of being wanted by this gorgeous, dominant man.

But then my mind goes and recalls what I saw on the internet. Nick with countless women on his arm.

I feel my stomach drop within me. Now that he's had me, now that the chase is over, will this be it?

"What's wrong, kitten?" he asks me as if he can sense my mood shifting.

"Nothing," I answer too quickly.

"Bullshit," he calls my bluff. "Tell me," he orders.

I hide my face in his chest, but he tuts and pulls my head up until my eyes have no choice but to meet his.

"As much as I love the feeling of you burrowing that pretty little red head into me, don't hide from me. What's bothering you?" Although his tone is gentle, it's stern too, letting me know that he's going to find out one way or another.

I sigh and just tell him the truth, "I don't want to be just another number in your long line of women."

He blinks in surprise. I've caught him off guard. He relaxes after a moment, pulling my head back to his chest and stroking his hands through my hair and down my back. I love the feeling of him petting me like this, but I'm fighting from totally melting into him.

"You're not just another woman to me," he says. "You're the *only* woman. All I want. All I need."

"But," I begin, "on the internet—"

He interrupts me, the irritation evident in his

voice, "The internet is full of lies, baby. Don't believe everything you see on it."

"So you're not one of Boston's most notorious playboys?"

His sardonic chuckle rumbles in his chest, "Is that the new moniker?"

"There are pictures of you with tons of women..." I trail off, unable to voice more.

He sighs and finally sits up, taking me with him.

When he helps me pull my shirt down and slides my panties and shorts onto me, my suspicions are all but confirmed. I was just another conquest. I'm asking too many questions like a needy girlfriend or something and now he's done with me.

I look down, unable to meet his eyes, feeling the tears pricking the backs of mine. I gave my virginity to a man who just wanted a fling.

I pull back when he tries to lift my face to his with a finger under my chin, but he's having none of it.

He captures my face with a hand on each cheek, making me look up at him.

His eyes are achingly soft when they look down at my moist ones, and he swears. I don't want him to feel sorry for me, though. I try to muster up the defiance I'm known for, but I can't. Not now.

"Daisy," he says my name tenderly, and I close my

eyes. "Look at me," he orders firmly. My eyes snap open at his command.

"What part of 'you're mine' do you not understand? I'm fucking obsessed with you. You're my everything. There is no other woman for me ever again. You're all I see, little hellcat."

I stare back at him, almost unable to believe what he's saying.

"Believe me," he orders as if he can read the doubts in my mind.

I nod my head, the heavy weight in the pit of my stomach lifting as I see the undeniable truth in his words.

He smiles as he sees my acceptance, leaning down to press his lips to mine.

Just as he starts to deepen the kiss, my tummy rumbles loudly, killing the mood.

I'm mortified at my body, but he pulls back and grins at me. "Hungry, kitten?"

I shrug sheepishly, "I haven't eaten anything but an apple all day."

He frowns down at me, "Let's get you fed then."

He stands, putting me eye level with his crotch. I can see the stain of my arousal on him from when he humped against me after telling me he came just from eating my pussy.

My face reddens and he grins wickedly, his thoughts there too, as he holds a hand down to me to help me up.

"Come on, kitten."

And like an obedient little pet, I move to obey.

***

Daisy

We walk back to my parents' house hand in hand. Nick slows his longer strides to match my smaller ones, and he periodically pulls our joined hands up to his lips to kiss my knuckles in a move so tender it makes my heart ache.

We're going to get in his car, and then he's going to drive us to his place where he already has a basket of food ready. Who knows if we'll actually take it out to the pond, though. At this point, I don't really care where we go so long as I'm with him.

When we reach the gate connecting our properties, my feet stall as I see flashing lights up ahead.

"Nick," I say tentatively, gripping his arm for support as I make out the shape of an ambulance up ahead.

Oh god. What's happened?

I can feel his frown as he tries to make out what's going on too.

Something is wrong with someone in my family. That's all I can think as I release his hand and go running toward home as fast as my feet can carry me.

Nick is right behind me.

When I finally reach the house, I see the paramedics wheeling my gran out on a stretcher.

"Gran?!" I scream as I go running up to them. I vaguely notice Dad standing with this arm wrapped around Mom. His face is grave and worried while Mom holds a hand up over her mouth, her eyes wet.

"What happened?" I ask them.

Mom shakes her head while Dad answers. "She just fell out in the floor. We called 9-1-1. She's breathing, but they've got to take her in for testing."

"Is anyone riding with her?" one paramedic asks.

I look to Dad, silently asking him for permission. I know he's her son, but I'm closer to Gran than anyone in this family. It should be me in there with her.

Dad nods, letting me know it's okay for me to go with her.

"I am," I volunteer, jumping into the back of the ambulance after they hoist her up.

I grab my grandmother's limp hand and hold it

between both of mine, tears streaming down my cheeks as I behold her pale face.

The last thing I see before the EMTs close the door of the ambulance is Nick comforting my parents.

Oh god, if my gran dies while I was out losing my virginity to Nick, how will I ever forgive myself?

CHAPTER EIGHT

Nick

DAISY WON'T ANSWER my texts. She won't take my calls.

I'made a quick trip to my house to change my slacks and then drove her parents to the hospital. Thankfully, her parents didn't notice the sex on my pants with all the commotion with the ambulance, but I didn't want to push my luck by not changing before offering to take them to the hospital.

Daisy had been monotone the whole time I'd been there. She'd let me touch her, but it was obvious she wasn't processing any comfort I or her parents tried to offer her.

She never left her grandmother's side. I stayed with her in the hospital that first night, but then she'd sent me home, telling me that she needed space. That her grandmother needed to be her primary concern and that while she appreciated my support, I was just a distraction.

I tried not to let her words hurt. I wanted to be there for her. But I also knew that after all the rail-roading I'd done, I needed to honor her request.

Turns out her grandmother had a stroke—a pretty serious one.

While Daisy might not accept my physical presence right now, I can't sit by and do nothing. So, I call in the best medical team money can buy and make sure her grandmother receives top-of-the-line care. The doctors keep me informed with progress reports, and I'm pleased at the progress Mrs. Cunningham is making. It's much quicker than that of a typical stroke victim, and I credit it both to the woman's vivacity and the excellent medical team.

And I continue to text and call Daisy every day. I leave her voicemails telling her I miss her and that I'm just a phone call away. I text her pictures of her pond and anything else I think she might like. While she never answers, I take comfort in the little tick mark on my phone showing me when she's read a message. She's at least reading what I send her.

I'm being patient—something that doesn't come naturally for me at all.

As much as I want Daisy right now, this time I'm waiting for her signal, respecting her wishes.

As much as it's killing me.

Daisy

"What are you still doing here, child?" Gran asks me.

I raise my head from where I had it laying on the side of her bed and smile at her. "Hey, Gran. You're awake."

"Of course I am," she fusses. Her speech is almost completely back to normal. It's unbelievable, but she has a great team of doctors and nurses. Thanks to Nick. My heart aches at just the thought of him, my feelings conflicted with longing and guilt.

"I wake up every day," Gran continues. "I'm doing fine. There's no need for you to sit here every minute of the day."

I shake my head at her, "Gran, I like being here with you. I'm not going to leave you alone."

My phone buzzes, but I ignore it. I'm pretty sure it's Nick, but I'll save his message to read when I can savor it later on when I get to missing him too much. After the first week, I was a bit surprised he still kept texting and calling me even when I couldn't bring myself to answer him. I was honestly half hoping, half afraid that he would get tired of me and give up, but he hasn't yet. He tries to contact me every day.

Sometimes his text messages are all that get me through the day.

When my phone buzzes again, Gran pins me with a look. "Go to him, Daisy."

"I don't know what you're talking about," I try to evade her.

"That man is crazy about you, and you're a fool if you don't see it," she says.

I look down at my hands where I pick at her comforter. "I don't want to leave you. I should have been there before when everything happened—not out on a date."

Gran cackles in that way of hers. "Jesus, child, is that what you're punishing yourself for? Hell, there was nothing you coulda done if you had been there.

Stop beating yourself up over that nonsense and go be with that man."

"But, Gran," I start to protest.

"I mean it, Daisy. Go live you life. I will not allow you to rot away in the hospital with me a moment longer. I'll have you kicked out if you don't leave."

"Gran!" I berate her, wide-eyed.

One look at her face, and I know she means business, though.

Her eyes soften as she regards me knowingly. "You remind me so much of myself when I was younger, you know..."

She reaches over to grasp my hand, though I notice her grip isn't as strong as it once was. "I know what it's like to be a wild thing that doesn't want to be caged, but, honey, there's nothing wrong with letting the *right* man tame you."

I look into my gran's wizened old eyes and listen to what she's saying. "Gran, I..."

"Do you love him?" she interrupts me.

I feel a lump in my throat. Do I love Nick? As impossible as it sounds, I know I do, but I don't know if he feels the same way. Yeah, he wants to possess me, but does that mean he loves me?

"I don't know if he feels the same way," I whisper, tears pricking my eyes.

"Ach," Gran scoffs. "Of course he does. A man doesn't pay for your ailing old gran's medical care if he doesn't plan on sticking around for the long haul."

I think about what she's said. "Maybe..." I concede slowly.

"Have I ever steered you wrong before?" she asks me with a delicate brow arched.

I shake my head.

"You're darn right I haven't," she confirms. "Now, go on. Get out of here."

I ponder what she's said. Maybe she's right, and either way, I'll never know if I keep hiding out here in the hospital with her. It's time to face the music.

I lean over and kiss her on the forehead. "Thanks, Gran. I love you. You call me if you need anything, okay? I'll make sure to keep my phone on me."

She motions me away with a wave of her hand.

Daisy

I'm a bundle of nerves as I pull up to Nick's house in my beat-up old truck—the same one that crapped out on me the day I met him.

I didn't tell him I was coming. I just jumped in the

truck and came straight here from the hospital before I lost my nerve.

Nick's door opens before I ever make it up the steps of his grand entryway.

He takes a couple of steps toward me and then stops himself. His hands curl into a fist and then flex slowly out. Every muscle in his body seems to be coiled tight like he's ready to spring at any moment.

He looks like a predator.

Dark and deadly, and I feel my heart speed up at the knowledge that he could so easily devour me.

"Hey," I say shyly.

"Hello, kitten," he greets me cautiously. He's standing stock still, but his eyes are blazing as they trail over me, devouring every inch of me with his eyes. If it's possible to have sex with your eyes, then consider me thoroughly fucked.

"How's your grandmother?" he asks me.

"Better." I nod my head. "She's doing much better. Thanks to you. Actually she's why I'm here."

His face falls somewhat, but he quickly masks it. "Does she need another type of treatment? Whatever she needs, if it's in my power to get it, I'll get it for her. You know that."

I shake my head and close the remaining steps between us. Taking a deep breath, I crane my neck to look up at him. We're so close I can feel the heat emanating off his body. Still, he makes no move to touch me.

I feel a moment of uncertainty. What if Gran was wrong? What if he doesn't feel the same way?

I look up into his golden eyes and steel my spine, knowing that I'll never know if I don't tell him. I've never backed down from anything before, and I'm not going to start now.

I muster up all the courage within me and then just blurt it out, "I love you, Nick."

There's a moment of complete silence during which the sound of the crickets chirping seems deafening.

"What did you say?" Nick asks the question so softly my face heats. I've probably freaked him out.

"I—" I fumble over my words. "I love you, but it's no big deal. You know, if you don't feel the same way."

I turn to start to run back to the safety of my truck, my face flaming with embarrassment. I can't believe what an utter fool I've made of myself, but suddenly his huge hand grabs my wrist, and he spins me back to face him.

He crushes me to his chest before his lips crash down onto mine. He kisses me desperately, his fingers tangling in my hair as he devours my mouth.

My body is instantly set aflame, and I cling to him.

"Oh, my angel," he whispers in between kisses. "My sweet, sweet kitten. If you only knew how much I've longed to hear you say that."

"You have?" I ask him breathlessly.

He chuckles. "I've been going crazy here waiting for you."

"So," I begin slowly. "Do you...?" I trail off, leaving the question hanging.

He laughs, a deep, masculine sound. "How could you not know? I love you, Daisy. With every fiber of my being. I've loved you from the moment you almost wrecked me over a goddamned turtle."

"Why didn't you tell me?" I huff at him. "I've been afraid you didn't feel the same way."

He laughs again. "You were always pissed at me for railroading you, remember? And you said you needed space after your gran's stroke. I was trying to do the right thing and let you come to me for once."

I shake my head at him. "*This* is what you choose to do the right thing on? Your logic is seriously twisted."

"I'll be honest with you," he tells me as he lopes his arms loosely around my waist. "I had about one day left in me, and then I was going to come get you come hell or high-water."

I raise a brow at him, "Hell or high-water? You been taking lessons from my daddy?"

He grins boyishly. "Some of his sayings are rubbing off on me. He's actually got a lot of good ones," he defends my father.

I laugh, and he swallows the sound with his mouth, kissing me for all he's worth.

My arms snake around his neck as his hands grip me under the thighs and haul me up into his arms. I instinctively wrap my legs around his waist as he carries me into his house, kicking the door shut behind us.

"Where are we going?" I ask him.

"To my bedroom," he growls. "I can't wait to have you sprawled out underneath me in my bed. I'm going to eat your pussy for an hour straight before I let you come, and then I'm going to fuck you all night long."

I feel the muscles he's talking about clench in need. I'm turned on beyond belief at the vivid picture he paints.

But when we get to his room and he throws me on the bed, I scramble to my knees and go for his belt as he quickly pulls his shirt from his body one-handed in that way that only men can do.

He growls when I finally unleash his cock. It

springs free right in front of my face, and I finally get to see it up close.

My eyes widen when I realize that *that's* what he put inside me. He's impossibly large and thick, and I don't see how he possibly fit.

He puts his hands under my arms and tries to pull me up, but I stop him. "No! I want to taste you," I tell him before I wrap my lips around his thick head, gathering the glistening drop of precum on his tip into my mouth.

"Fuck, you're going to kill me," he groans, throwing his head back as I swirl my tongue tentatively around the tip of him. He's hard yet velvety smooth, and he tastes salty and musky.

He only lets me explore for a few more minutes before he drags me up the bed and settles his body on top of mine. "Can't take it, baby. Your mouth feels too good," he rasps against my neck before he suckles the sensitive flesh into his mouth, laving it with his tongue.

He only pulls back long enough to rip my tank top over my head. He unclasps my bra and flings it to the side too. Then, he makes quick work of my shorts and panties before his mouth is suddenly everywhere, all over me.

When he finally settles between my legs, he grins

up at me wickedly. "An hour, kitten. I've got an hour to feast on this pretty pussy of yours."

"Nick!" I cry out as soon as his lips touch me. He suckles my clit, his tongue swirly expertly over the bud. He alternates between swirling, flicking and laving his tongue over it. He goes maddeningly slow, and then he picks up the pace until I'm ready to explode, and then he backs off again.

I don't know how long he keeps up his torture, bringing me to the brink of ecstasy only to ebb off again, but it feels like forever, so maybe he really does eat me out for an hour. I'm a sobbing, whining mess, babbling incoherently as I plead for relief before he finally gives me what I need.

"Come for me," he orders before he sucks hard on my clit one last time, expertly swirling his tongue on my swollen, over-sensitized bud, and I shatter.

I fucking shatter.

White light pops behind my eyes as I scream out something that's supposed to be his name. My entire body feels like it's falling apart. The rush of pleasure is so intense it takes my breath away.

When I come back to my senses, Nick is holding himself on top of me, gazing down at me adoringly.

"There you are," he whispers, stroking my face.

I can still feel my legs trembling as he lifts them up and wraps them around his waist.

"You're so beautiful when you fall apart in my arms like that, baby. I want to watch you do that every night for the rest of our lives," his voice is husky as he says it.

Warmth fills me at his words, and I want nothing more than the pretty picture he paints of a life with him. "I love you, Nick," I whisper.

"I love you too, baby. Don't you ever doubt it again," he tells me as he pushes into me, holding my eyes the entire time as he fills me.

I feel him stretching me impossibly wide. While it doesn't hurt as much as last time, it still burns as he fills me.

He never stops his progress, though, pushing steadily into me until he's fully seated inside me.

"Fuuuuck," he groans out when he finally bottoms out in me. His breathing is already heavier, and I love the way he looks, his muscles hard and bunched with the effort it takes him to hold back, his neck straining.

"Take me," I tell him as I wrap my arms around his neck, giving myself to him completely.

"Fuck, Daisy, you're mine, you know that?" he says as he begins to pump into me furiously.

"Yes!" I moan out as he hits this spot deep inside

me that causes flutters to begin to take root low in my belly.

I arch up into him, seeking more, and he catches on quickly, keeping his hips angled so that he keeps hitting that spot over and over again inside me.

"You like that, kitten?" he rasps as he drags his cock in and out of me.

"Yes! Yes! Please don't stop!" my nails are clawing at his back as he pummels that delicious spot inside me over and over again. I'm moaning louder with each thrust, and then I feel him swelling inside me.

"Fuck, I'm coming!" he cries out as he slams deep one last time. I scream as my world falls apart. I feel my pussy clenching around him violently, and then I feel his warm heat pulsing into me.

Without ever pulling out of me, he rolls onto his back, dragging me with him so that I'm laying on top of him.

He strokes my hair from my face until I can feel the long strands falling onto the small of my back as he covers my face with tiny kisses.

"Mine," he whispers against my forehead.

"Yours," I whisper against his chest.

Always.

EPILOGUE

Five Years Later

Nick

"NO, LIKE THIS, SILLY," I hear my wife's musical laughter floating through the air as she sits by the pond with our five-year-old boy, Derrick, trying to teach him how to properly bait his own fishing hook.

My son's boyish giggles fill the air, too. My two favorite sounds in the world.

He has his mother's red hair, but his golden eyes are all mine. I already know he's going to have the girls swooning when he gets older with his unique color combination.

It's a good thing I like to move fast because no sooner were we married than Daisy found out she was pregnant. Of course, I pushed her to marry me just two weeks after she told me she loved me. Fortunately, I had her whole family on board with the idea too, especially her grandmother. I owe that woman everything for convincing Daisy to open up to me. She'll live out the rest of her days in luxury if I have anything to say about it. Daisy and I visit her often and make sure she has everything she needs, and of course, the old woman thinks her great-grandson hangs the moon and the sun.

I wouldn't be surprised if Daisy and I conceived our son the first time we made love here by this very pond.

I feel my dick twitching in my pants just thinking about it.

Before our son was born, I took her on damn near every surface of the house and every space I could find to safely take her outdoors. My woman will always be a tomboy at heart, and I love indulging that wild side of her and fuck her in the great outdoors every chance I get. Though I did put my foot down at her climbing trees. She damn near gives me a heart attack every time she does it. I'm terrified she's going to fall. Of course, she doesn't fucking listen. She's disobedient as hell, but I wouldn't have her any other way. Her free spirit just gives me a chance to punish her. I swear I think she acts out on purpose just because she loves our little games as much as I do.

I'm happy to say I've officially been removed from Boston's most eligible billionaire bachelor's list, though I can't say that's stopped the paparazzi's interest in me. Fortunately, we don't have to deal with that much out here where we live in our own little bubble, but I do occasionally have to make a trip to the city, and I always have my gorgeous little redheaded wife on my arm when I do.

True to my desires the first day I ever saw her, I bought her a pretty little Mercedes and have dripped her in aquamarine diamonds and designer labels. She says she doesn't need any of those things, but that's exactly why I want to give them to her. She asks for nothing. Nothing but me, so I want to give her the world.

"Daddy! Daddy! Look!" I hear splashing coming from the pond and glance over from where I sit musing on the blanket I laid out early this morning when we first walked over to the pond.

"I caught one!" My boy is holding his line up

proudly, the fish flopping at end of his hook. I walk over to him to get a better look.

"That's great, bud!" I ruffle his hair. "What do you say we throw him back?"

"Okay!" Derrick readily agrees. While we some-times eat the fish he and Daisy catch, this one is way too small to be a keeper.

Daisy's reeling her line in and packing up. The sun is getting higher in the sky as it gets closer to noontime. The fish never bite in the middle of the day, she quickly taught me. The best time to fish in this part of the country is early in the morning and late in the evening.

"You ready to go, kitten?" I ask her.

"Yeah," she smiles at me. She looks just as mouth-watering as the day I first met her. While I like to deck her out in designer labels, she still wears an old pair of cut-off shorts and a tank top when we come out fishing to the pond. Her red hair is gathered up in a messy ponytail on the top of her head, and I swear all I can think about is holding onto it as I ride her from behind when I get her on all fours.

Derrick laughs and looks up at me curiously. "Why do you always call mama, kitten, daddy? She's not a kitty, silly."

My eyes meet Daisy's over his head, and we share

a look. Mine is full of everything I want to do to her, I'm sure. Her cheeks flush, and I remind myself that I might need to keep that particular nickname for my wife more private now that my son is getting older.

Derrick is completely tuckered out after we make our way back to the house, so I put him down for a nap as Daisy gets cleaned up.

Thankfully, he's out as soon as his head touches the pillow.

I leave his room with a singular purpose in mind, making my way to the bedroom I share with Daisy as quick as my feet will carry me.

I hear the water from the shower still going when I reach our room, and I waste no time in shucking out of my clothes and joining her under the spray.

I come up behind her and wrap her in my arms, pulling her back flush against my front, letting her feel what she does to me pressing against her sweet little ass.

She grinds her ass against me, teasing me, but she has no idea what she's doing. I'm too wound up to endure her torture today. A stream of cum jets out of my cock and lands on her back at the titillating contact.

"Don't tease me, hellcat," I whisper right into her ear.

"Hmm, which is it? Kitten or hellcat?" she hums as

she tilts her head back to allow me access to her throat in an open invitation. I don't need her to ask twice. I lower my lips to the smooth column and lave my tongue over her like an animal, sending tremors throughout her body as she melts against me.

"Both," I answer before I bite down on her neck. She gasps, her hand coming up behind her to wrap around the nape of my neck and pull me closer.

I bend my hips to press the tip of my erection against her wetness and ram into her with one hard thrust.

Holding her throat with one hand and her hip with the other, I begin to work myself in and out of her. She always feels so much tighter from this angle, and I know I won't last long.

Her back is arched, her body perfectly bowed for me as I pound into her relentlessly.

Her whimpers are sounding all around us as the steam from the shower consumes us.

"Jesus Christ, Daisy," I rasp as I feel her tight channel sucking and milking me as she comes.

Two more pumps, and I groan out my own release, shoving my cum as deep inside her as I get it.

My woman is everything. She's fire and ice. She burns with her sass, but she goes down smooth like Tennessee whiskey.

And best of all? She's fucking mine.

THE END

More from Emma Bray

Connect with Emma!

Visit Emma's website to get a FREE book you can't get anywhere else: www.authoremmabray.com.

9 7 9 8 2 1 5 9 4 2 2 0 8